FALLEN HALOS

CURSED ANGEL WATCHTOWER 1

ERIN HAYES
REBECCA HAMILTON

EVERSTORM

ABOUT THE CURSED ANGEL COLLECTION

Angels and Witches must join forces to overcome the Demons that have cursed the earth.

Many years ago, a demon inhabited a witch's body to cast a spell to open all thirteen dimensions so that the demon spirits trapped there could be unleashed onto earth. But when the demons were released, the dimensions collided, creating rifts in the earth that re-divided the world into 13 continents, each with their own curse.

In each city, high and protected in the city's Watchtower, the Demon Lord of that dimension resides. And so long as that Demon remains on earth, his curse will reign over the Circle where he resides. In an attempt to reverse the damage, 13 of the strongest angels were sent to earth to defeat the Demon Lords. However, their sacrifice came at a price: they would have to take on the curse of the circle they were sent to, and would be damned to earth until the curse was lifted.

Lifting the curse, however, means befriending a witch… whom the angels believe to all be as evil as the demons themselves.

CHAPTER 1

W*ake up, Rahym.*
No, I don't want to.

I want to curl in on myself, rock myself to a blissful, dreamless sleep, and never wake up again. Is that too much to ask? I can't stand thinking. Then again, I can't stand standing for too long without collapsing after a time.

So go do something with that time. Anything. You have a million and one things to do that you never get around to. Forget the curse. Just do something.

Yes, too true. I'm always right, even when I don't want to be.

I open my eyes.

And I'm still in the same goddamn place.

Well, what did you expect? It's not like you can click your heels and be sent to a better place.

I read about that in an old book about wizards and scarecrows and an emerald city once. If only I could do something like that. Magic exists, but magic never helps humans like me.

As it is, I'm stuck.

We're all stuck.

"Well, that's just fan-fucking-tastic, isn't it?" I mutter out loud, and Yusup, one of my hired guards sitting near the door, opens one eye at me before closing it again.

Saving energy. Smart man.

Meanwhile, I am not a smart man.

I'm behind the counter in the Great Room of my Lodge, a resting place for anyone who is worried about their safety when the Sleep overtakes them. It's nothing special—just a large, two-story clay and brick building that has been crumbling for over fifty years. It was built *before* the curse; no one in their right mind would expend the effort to build such a structure these days. Beds line the walls with old sofas scattered about the center of the room. A flight of stairs leads to the second floor where there are more beds and recliners. I've discounted those rooms for anyone who wants to waste energy climbing the stairs.

Yes, we're so desperate that we're counting our footsteps. The silver lining is that the beds are *really* nice upstairs for anyone who pays half-price. I try to sleep there whenever I can myself. And I pay double to any of my staff who are willing to put their energy to go upstairs and clean.

I drum my fingers on the torn arms of my overstuffed recliner. An energy waste, but I have plenty of tics like that. A lot of the foam and cushion has come through at the seams, and the footrest no longer works, but I don't have the energy or the care to fix it.

Well, you could...

With an average of four hours a day to do even the most menial tasks—depending on how much effort I put into them—I need to save as much strength as possible. Some people compare the curse to a bucket of water. Imagine waking up every day in the desert with that bucket half-full of water.

Everything you do that day requires spoonfuls of water to varying degrees. Larger tasks require more water. Smaller ones require less. And once you're out of water, you can't move, you can't blink, you aren't even conscious most of the time.

If you're able to pace yourself, you can extend yourself to last through the entire day.

Most people find that just living only gives them four hours of energy, though. I'm one of them.

So reupholstering an old recliner is pretty low on my to-do list.

You know what's on your to-do list, Rahym. Moping isn't one of them.

The thought slips unbidden into my subconscious, and the only good part about it is that it distracts me enough to not think about the past again. Rather, I'm now thinking about the present and the very-near future.

That's all I can do. That's all anyone can do.

"You know what I hate the most about this damn curse?" I say to Yusup across the room.

He pries an eye open but doesn't answer. It's pretty common for that to happen, so I don't take offense to it, and even if he did mean offense, I'm his boss, so I speak anyway.

"It's that our energy resets at midnight. 12:01 rolls around, and it's like, 'Goody, I have seven hours 'til sunrise.' And I try not to use up my energy, but I just feel like doing something. Like nighttime hiking or streaking or *something*." I frown wistfully. "It feels like a lot of our time is wasted on the night. Imagine if our energy reset at sunrise. You'd wake up, refreshed. Like the world's best damn cup of Chal."

Yusup snorts through his nose, the closest thing I'll get to a laugh from him. He's so quiet most of the time, I almost forget he's there. I think he has an easier job of clearing his mind. He's a big man who spends half his days weightlifting and half his days being a guard at my Lodge. The pay is good, and he has no family to speak of, so he'll do this gig until he meets a girl he'll want to provide for.

I had a future like that once. I took a dangerous job as a miner, and I worked to save up as much money as possible for a dowry. And we were happy, for a time.

Before my wife and daughter were killed.

I still remember how my body went into Hibernation before I could save my family. All I could do was lay there on the ground, body unmoving, eyes unblinking, the flames burning my retinas, the screams piecing my eardrums, and all I wanted was for me to fall into unconsciousness...

Shh. Stop, Rahym.

I'm right, I need to stop. Focus on something else. Like that damn to-do list.

I pull it out of my pocket, a tattered piece of paper with a good three dozen things to do. I've arranged them in order of priority. Unfortunately, most days, once I get past number four, my energy is done, and I go into the Sleep. Numbers one through four *always* have to be done. Every damn day.

1. *Delegate tasks to the staff.*
2. *Turn over all the beds.*
3. *Greet the guests and place them in appropriate rooms.*
4. *Do a perimeter walk to make sure that the firebreaks are clear.*

THAT LAST ONE is an absolute necessity, seeing that we're so close to the Door to Hell. Wildfires are a daily threat here, so letting my guard down, even for one second, can cost lives. I learned that at the expense of my…

Stop it, Rahym.

Right. Yes, stay focused on the task at hand.

I go down to number nineteen, one that I haven't been able to get to in three years. Something has always happened or gotten in the way. They've all been excuses, sure, but when I have a set amount of energy each day, there are plenty of things I'd rather do than number nineteen.

19)DIG UP the remains of THE tree

IT'S BEEN an eyesore at the front of the Lodge for three years, and I really need to remove it. A hulking, charred tree trunk that's nearly as tall as the Lodge itself. The more intrepid, curious travelers who aren't terrified of expending their energy have asked what happened to it. I haven't been able to answer them.

It was the fig tree that Maysa planted when she was a child. It was the tree that I carved our initials in when we were married and I promised to always take care of her. It was the tree that caught fire when she and our daughter died.

I could have had one of my workers, like Yusup, remove it. Yet something always stopped me. It hasn't escaped me that I've put it off for a variety of reasons. I don't want to let go. I don't want to relive that moment. I don't want to lose that last piece. Removing that tree is something I need to do for closure, and I don't *want* closure.

Well, you're feeling feisty today, aren't you?

"Apparently, I am," I mutter to myself. Again, Yusup raises an eyebrow, but he's used to my mutterings by now.

In one swift movement, I get up from my spot on the recliner, lift up the access to the counter, and head to the front door.

"Boss?" Yusup asks, curious. After all, I've already done my daily perimeter check. This is out of the norm for me. It's out of the norm for any sane person.

I feel like I'm about to do something dastardly, which is a far cry from the despair that I should be feeling. I embrace it and offer him a wide smile.

"Just gonna do number nineteen," I tell him. "It's time."

Yusup pauses, knowing exactly what number nineteen is. After all, he's seen it on my to-do list for the past three years. "But—"

I don't even let him waste the energy to say any more. "Stay here and watch the guests. I may be out for a while."

"Do you—"

"Yes, I've been conserving my energy all day. If I start to get tired, I'll come in." Because being left outside the Lodge, unattended and unprotected, is just asking for me to be killed. Which isn't a bad thing to ask.

If you ask me.

Don't confuse yourself again.

Right.

I blink and smile again. "I'll be fine, Yusup."

The big man frowns. Good. I'm glad to know I have staff who genuinely care for me. "If you start—"

I wave him away. "Yes, if I start to feel too tired to come in, I'll call for you."

I don't expect that to happen, though. I'm too stubborn to be killed, or at least I'm too stubborn to admit otherwise. I give him an absent pat before I slip out the front door to the outside.

It's nearly nine-thirty at night, and I'm alone in the

desert. Still two-and-a-half hours until my strength is replenished for another day.

Maybe you can do number twenty tomorrow.

Let's not get crazy now.

The smell of ash and fire is strong on the wind tonight, meaning that the wind is coming out of the northwest. The Door to Hell must be in full inferno tonight. The Demon Lord is cooking up something malicious, even if his Watchtower is miles and miles away. Not that any human has survived the trek through the Door to Hell to see his Watchtower in person.

It's just legends and hearsay at this point.

I sniff the air and turn toward it, seeing the orange glow just over the crest of a dune. It's stronger than normal tonight, and I can see the tips of flames lick the sky.

"Well, aren't you an ugly bastard?" I ask the Door.

The Door to Hell isn't necessarily a "Door," so to speak. It's a wasteland, uninhabitable for most any creature, human or otherwise. What's more, it burns constantly.

While the outer edge of the Door is seven miles away, my Lodge is the closest anyone dares to stay. A few more intrepid souls have risked living closer—after all, the area surrounding the Door is rich in natural gases, so they'll try working there to earn good money in the hopes that one day they can live farther away, where it's safe.

Or safer, anyway. You're never really safe when you can smell the fires from the Door.

There was once even a village fewer than two miles from the Door. It burned to a crisp about ten years ago, if that tells you anything.

The road that passes by the Lodge is a well-traveled one. To the southwest of me is Derweze, the closest town. The Devil's Teeth Mountains flank the east side of the Lodge, impassable unless you want to traverse ten days around the range. And with the curse the way it is, to do that is just as dangerous as being this close to the Door. To the northeast is the town of Merv, which is built around an ancient oasis from the times of the Silk Road. To travel between Derweze and Merv, you have to travel fifteen miles in the desert. Most people can't travel that distance in four hours unless they're marathon runners, and even then, they'll expend their energy long before they get to safety. Horses are impacted by the curse as well, and both the rider and the beast would be stranded before they reached their destination, even if the horse were a legendary Turkmen Akhal-Teke.

That's why my Lodge is here. It's the midway point between the two towns, giving travelers a rest stop. The Devil's Teeth arch over the building, shielding it from the fires spewing from the Door. It's some semblance of protection, at least.

Yet there are other dangers that threaten our lives all the time.

Such as me standing here, talking to the Door like it will talk back. It won't, right?

Of course not. To-do list, Rahym.

Right. Must get back to the to-do list. Number nineteen.

I turn my head to see the remains of the tree. It looks even more sinister now than I remember, and it looks a hell of a lot more daunting, too. The trunk twists up on itself, reaching with huge branches to the sky, as if celebrating the fires burning only a few miles away.

It never used to be this ugly. It was once beautiful, a fig tree that grew in the middle of the desert. Maysa could make anything blossom and flourish here. That was her gift—a light that's now gone, replaced by the constant glow of embers on the horizon.

I let out a shuddering breath, getting rid of the despair that's building up within me at these thoughts. I can't go there. Just keep moving. Keep living.

Good, Rahym.

"Thank you," I say, straightening up. I feel much better, having let go of that negative energy. Still a bit off, but that's my general state these days. I embrace it.

"You look like you're going to take more than I've got energy for," I say to the tree. No wonder I've been putting it off. It's going to take me weeks to remove it. Months, if there's a sudden surge of travelers to the Lodge.

"I'll go get the shovel. Stay right here."

I head to the side of the building to the shed that houses all of the landscaping equipment. Really, we don't landscape here, because we have packed sand and unusable dirt. But we use the shovels to dig and redig the trenches surrounding the Lodge as firebreaks, and while it would be nice to leave the shovels out (it uses energy to go get the shovels from the shed and put them back), demonlings would steal them if we did that.

I unlock the shed, grab a shovel and, after thinking about it, pick out a hatchet to hack the damn tree if need be. I make sure to lock up again before I tread back to the front, determined to fulfill my task.

And I'm not alone anymore.

I can see movement to the south, silhouetted by the flickering glow from the Door. Several shapes move along the dunes at a fast clip. I know it's not a group of animals—this dry, arid wasteland can't sustain more than small lizards, tarantulas, and the bones of those unlucky enough to get caught by the desert. The only other thing it could be is a demonling, and they're part of the reason why it's so dangerous to live here.

My hand reaches to my hip, grasping for a pistol that I stupidly forgot back inside.

Whoopsies.

"Dammit," I mutter.

Rookie mistake. I have the hatchet, so that will have to serve as weapon if it comes down to it.

No one comes to my Lodge at this time of night. Most travelers have already expended their day's energy by now.

My first instinct is that it is a group of demonlings. *Bastards.* If they attack us now, there's no way that I'll be much help. I have a few other hired hands that are fresher and will be able to defend the Lodge until midnight. But it's always a risk, and judging by the size of this group, we wouldn't make it.

As the group comes closer, I see that they're all riding horses. I know from experience that demonlings and horses don't mix—they tend to eat the horses—so my fear of danger eases, but just slightly.

They must be more guests, then. Where's your sense of propriety?

I must have locked it up at the shed behind the Lodge. I hide the hatchet behind my back as I step into the loose sand of the Karakum Desert, heading toward them. I note that with every step out into the open air, I have to take that many steps back.

That could be a problem if I take too many steps one way.

But these travelers are human. And it's my duty to help them if they need it. Otherwise, they could very well die out here. And I might not have the energy to move their bodies. It'd be bad for business.

I clear my throat. "Stop right there!"

To my relief, the group slows about fifty yards from me. I count a dozen, noting that it's a mix of riders on horses and runners on foot with pack mules carrying supplies. Based on their bulky appearances, I'm guessing that they're all wearing armor. And that they're probably armed to the teeth.

Definitely not the latest fashion craze from Derweze.

Who are these people?

"State your name and your purpose," I tell them.

"Rahym? Rahym Tezel? Is that you?"

I still, recognizing the voice. The memories seem to physically hit me, sucking the air out of my lungs.

"Yes, it's me," I say warily. "Who are you?"

Please don't let it be him. Please don't… both my subconscious and I chant.

I really don't want to deal with that asshole right now. Or ever again, for that matter.

I get my answer. One of the riders dismounts, landing in the sand. He lifts his hood back and looks at me, his emerald green eyes glowing with unearthly power. The sharp planes of his face are exaggerated by the light from the Door as he gives me a lopsided smile.

Goddammit.

"Nakir," I say with a false sense of bravado, and I wish I were seeing him under different circumstances. I'm sure he can smell my armpits as I haven't showered in over a week— that's number five on any good day. "What are you doing here?"

The smile grows as a second rider swings a leg over the side of his horse. The rider strides up next to the asshole that I blame for the shattered remains of my life. This much closer, I can see that it's a woman, although she doesn't lift her hood, so I can't see her face.

"We're on the road, Rahym," Nakir says, drawing my attention back to him. "And we need your help."

"*My* help?" I ask.

He nods.

"I'm flattered, but I don't do that anymore. People tend to die around you."

To my surprise, the woman next to Nakir chuckles mirthlessly. Shit, she may be crazier than I am. Not a good sign.

Nakir smirks. "Dying. Right. That's exactly why we need you, Rahym."

"Why?"

Nakir exchanges a glance with the woman. She pulls back her hood as well, and from the depths of my memory, I recall *her*.

Shit.

Well, this night has taken an unexpected turn.

"Jennet," I say, calling out her name. It's been years, and the last time I saw her was when we were teenagers. She disappeared just after her father died many years ago, so it may not be here. The curve of her lips tells me that I identified her correctly.

A new sort of horror overtakes me; what is Jennet doing with Nakir?

"Hello, Rahym," she says in a clear voice. "We're going to lift the curse. And we need you to lead us through the Door to Hell."

CHAPTER 2

N^{o.}
For once, my inner voice and I agree.

"No," I whisper aloud, feeling much like a sand lizard trapped between two walls of fire. I've seen it happen before —it didn't end well for the lizard. Much like this crazy vendetta that Nakir and Jennet are talking about. I've tried it. Seen what happens when you try it.

And it always ends with charred bodies.

"No," I say again, louder this time. "That's—"

"A lost cause?" Nakir raises an eyebrow as if amused by my sudden tied tongue. He always did have a warped sense of humor, the bastard. I'm telling them how crazy this is, and here he is, smirking at me. Jennet, too.

"Fucking insane," I tell him. "Are those…" I nod toward the group behind them. Afraid of what they are, even though I know it.

He nods. "Halos."

Your old group.

I lick my lips, my eyes darting between each of them. "I don't recognize any of them."

"That's because you don't know them," Nakir says.

I laugh—actually *laugh* at that. Nakir and Jennet exchange *that* glance again, and I wonder when they became so buddy-buddy. I had no idea that Nakir knew Jennet. Or why, out of all the Lodges in Turkmenistan surrounding the Door to Hell, they had to come to mine.

And out of all the possible schmucks they could have approached, they chose me. Surely there are others who know the Door to Hell like I do.

"I know what you're thinking, Rahym," Nakir says placatingly.

I shake my head. "You have no idea."

He waves me off. "We really have a chance this time. We've got a secret weapon."

"A magic wand?" Because that's all that I can think of that would get them through the Door to Hell. And that requires a fairy godmother and a list of good karma out the ass.

Neither of which Nakir has.

"No. *Her.*" He points to the woman at his side.

"Jennet?" I ask, certain that can't be right. "How is…? What makes her…?" My mind stumbles across the thoughts and implications. "How is *she* a secret weapon?"

Even in the darkness, I can see that she flushes at my assessment. "That is a story best told in private," she says, casting a furtive glance around us.

"And you expect me to give you a private place?"

You do have room, my mind tells me.

Shut up.

"For an old friend," Nakir says, as if feeding off my traitorous brain. "Yes."

14

No.

He's not throwing that "old friend" business on me. We may have been friends in the past, but friends don't disappear on you when your family dies. Friends don't come back and pretend like it's all okay.

Because it sure as hell isn't.

Nakir seems to finally understand that I'm not budging. He sighs and combs a hand through his hair. "Hear us out, Rahym. And if you still don't like what we have to say, you can kick us back out on the road, and we'll figure something else. You owe me that much."

I snarl. "I don't owe you anything."

He clears his throat, visibly caught off guard. "No, you don't. But I owe you. I misspoke."

I want to tell him that he has misspoken about a great many things in our times together. Mainly about false hope and prophecies and this idea that if we head into the Door to Hell and kill the Demon Lord Abaddon, we can lift the curse. It's all bullshit, and it costs more than people's lives. It costs the hopes and dreams of those left behind.

Tell him like it is, Rahym. I'm egging myself on now, wanting to start something. Usually that gets me into trouble.

Then again, Nakir is nothing but trouble, and while he was wrong about me owing him my time, I do owe him a piece of what's left of my mind.

I even open my mouth to do so when Jennet steps forward and gently puts a hand on my shoulder. The touch grounds me, and I look at her, shocked at her close proximity. We haven't seen each other in years, and my memory must be hazy of her, because there's no way she was as beautiful then as she is now.

Then again, the last time I saw her was when we were thirteen years old. We grew up in the same village, too close to the Door to Hell, but also so achingly close to the place where we knew we could lift the curse. Back then, Jennet was all legs with too little on her bones, and she often traveled with my family to deliver supplies.

Now, the woman looking back me beneath the folds of her hood is startlingly stunning. Smooth, olive skin. High cheekbones framing a proud nose, with square, luscious lips. Intelligent, azure eyes watch me, pleading with me. A wisp of dark hair has fallen in her dirt-stained face. She's dirty from her travels, but it only seems to enhance what's already there.

Like a diamond in the rough.

Stop staring.

I clear my throat, and I'm about ready to speak—even though questions fly through my head at the moment, mainly what happened to her?—when I hear something heavy collapse to the dirt.

The three of us startle, looking at the group that are accompanying Nakir and Jennet. I almost forgot they were there.

"Who was it?" Nakir demands tiredly.

"Nury," a young woman's clear voice rings out, a touch of panic to her words. "The Hibernation overtook him." I get a better look at this Nury guy. He's a tall, wiry man, slight of build and strength, apparently.

There's a stillness to the group, as we are all reminded that we're expending energy standing here, talking. They're waiting for me to either turn them away or to invite them into the Lodge.

And, to be honest, I don't know what's right. Letting them in would be inviting disaster back into my life. But turning them away may be sentencing some of them to death, if any more are as close to Hibernation as this Nury fellow was.

16

Nakir looks back at me, his eyes pleading. *"Please,* Rahym."

I glance at Jennet, who is also watching me, and I realize that I can't do it. I can't turn them away. "Come inside," I say. "There are warm beds and sofas for you. Replenish your strength." I give Nakir a hard look. "Don't you dare say anything to my staff about who you are. Or *what* you are."

Nakir sighs, and I can feel the relief traveling through the whole group. Well, the ones that are conscious, at least. Nury is still on the ground like a forgotten log.

"Thank you," Nakir whispers.

He brushes past me and singlehandedly picks up the man who collapsed and carries him back to the Lodge as if he's a sack of potatoes.

You've forgotten what it's like to be around Nakir.

"Not entirely," I whisper. I haven't forgotten the most important pieces about that.

Jennet smiles gratefully, and as her hand leaves my shoulder, I can feel its lingering touch. I close my eyes, wondering if this is wise.

But I promised that I would help travelers in need. And this is a group of travelers in need. I don't have to like it, but I promised Maysa I would do it.

"Yusup!" I yell. "Come take these horses to the stable."

As they enter my Lodge, I can't help but wonder why Nakir is here. Why he thinks I give a damn about helping him again, after the last time.

He's a fallen angel, after all. And the last time he tried killing the Demon Lord and removing the curse, we both nearly died. And even now, I wish I were with those who did die.

17

CHAPTER 3

Ko vacancy. *It's been a long time since you had that.*

"Yeah," I mutter. Since long before the village of Darvaza was destroyed in a fire.

No one hears me, though. The Halos all fall into Hibernation soon after entering the Lodge. I didn't realize they were so close to collapse when they arrived.

Nothing is more dangerous than going into Hibernation outside at night. If ten people had collapsed, I'm not sure my staff would have had the strength to bring them in.

They fill up most of the remaining couches on the bottom floor. As they haven't cleaned themselves from their travels and they're not paying for their rooms—Nakir never did like dealing with money, the bastard, so I don't expect to see one coin from him—I'm not about to put them up in one of the good beds.

It still feels like I'm moving through a dream. That this is not really happening. I've had some crazy, messed-up dreams when Hibernation took me, but nothing like this.

"Thank you again," Nakir says with a long sigh as he sits on a recliner in the Great Room. A few feet away, Jennet is curled up on a daybed herself, stone cold and passed out to the world. Nakir himself looks like he's nearly at the end of his strength, too.

The curse even affects the likes of a fallen angel.

That always amazed me. That such a strong, able-bodied creature could still be affected by the curse.

"Don't thank me," I say, crossing my arms as I appraise him quietly. He winces as he leans back, and I nod at him. "Do the stubs of your wings still hurt?"

He purses his lips a moment before answering. "They still bleed."

I nod. "Right. I remember that now. You always wore bandages to keep the blood at bay."

He raises an eyebrow. "It's been a while, Rahym."

"Not long enough." I spit out the words like they're fire. "You can stay until morning. But then I want you out. Gone. *Kaput.*"

Don't be that way.

I can be any way I want. It's my Lodge.

I turn to head out the front door.

"You're not going with us?" Nakir asks behind me.

I scowl back at him. "Your new group of *Halos* interrupted me when I was trying to mark number nineteen off my list," I tell him.

I may have another hour's worth of strength left in me yet, and midnight is right around the corner. The shovel is outside; I can make a start on digging up the tree.

I leave him there and go out into the night air again. Even though it's colder outside, I can still feel the heat in my cheeks as I pick up my shovel and hatchet and start hammering at the tree, using up my strength too quickly and too haphazardly to really be effective.

I just feel like I need to destroy something.

CHAPTER 4

M y work on the tree did nothing. I can't even see a dent in it the next morning, and I don't feel better for having tried to remove it. It makes me feel jittery, as if there's something not done. Maybe because that's exactly the issue. It's *not* done. After years of completing tasks one through four, not having completed something I've started takes me aback.

Blame it on Nakir.

Oh, I am. Trust me.

Morning is nowhere near as frightening as the night, but that doesn't make it any less dangerous. From my spot in the Great Room, I can see the dust trail of something moving through the Karakum desert. Something fast, at a faster clip than even horses.

Demonlings. Stirring up trouble.

We may have to deal with that later. As it is at the moment, I need to conserve strength.

Just in case.

I frown unhappily and return my attention to Nakir and

Jennet. The other travelers in their group are still curled up in their beds, saving themselves for the day ahead.

Because based on this meeting, they may be out on the road again.

Nakir is watching me with an amused smirk on his perfect face. As it's sometime after eight in the morning, the morning light makes him look as though he's some sort of sun god. The angel may have been a fallen one, but he's no less a thing of perfection. Even as a widowed, straight man, I can see the appeal of Nakir, and I know that a great many women (and men) have fallen under his spell.

I've never met another angel, fallen or otherwise, but I assume they're all the same. They have the look that they're chiseled from marble, beautiful creatures, looking at me hopefully now.

No, it's just Nakir doing that.

And Jennet.

I pointedly try not to look at her, but it's hard. While Nakir is a being to be admired, Jennet looks both ethereal and human in her appearance. It's a contrast to him, and it's one that I want to gravitate toward, because he's just so damn blindingly perfect.

And she's…well, she's Jennet.

I clear my throat. "Speak."

Exhaustion from last night gave me one nugget of mercy, and I agreed to hear him out, even though I told him vehemently that I doubted anything he said would fix it.

Nakir arches an eyebrow before he leans forward and sighs. He combs his hands through his hair—*That means he's nervous, right?*—before speaking.

"Where do I even start?"

"Where *do* you start?" I repeat. Annoyance pinches at the back of my head, and I gesture helplessly, trying to feed him prompts. "How about the thing you're doing. What you're doing with the Halos. Why you want me. And what you're doing with Jennet."

"Heh." He smirks. "You make it seem easy, Rahym. We both know nothing is easy."

Including his logic. Then again, my logic isn't very good right now, either. I tell it to shush. It does, thankfully.

"Just tell me what you're doing here."

Nakir exchanges a glance with Jennet one more time before speaking. "We're here to break the curse."

I nod. "You told me that. You do realize that our curse makes it impossible to break the very same curse, right? That's the whole point of it. Hell, you even told me that when we first met."

He laughs. "Too true. But we may have found a loophole. And we need you to help."

I shake my head. "You already tried doing that with me once, and look where it ended up."

"And here you are now," he says. *"Alive."*

That makes two of us.

Right. Yes. *Only* two of us. I wag a finger at him. "You and I are the only members of the original Halos here. Is that because the rest of them died?" I remember Sasha. Onsen. And so many more. My friends. The color drains from Nakir's face. A very human reaction, which makes me hate him even more.

Because he's feeling remorse for those deaths, but he's about to risk it one more goddamned time. And this time he's bringing Jennet into it.

She'll die.

Suddenly, I don't want my childhood friend to follow everyone else into death. Not if I can help it. And I know very well how I can drive that home.

"Do these new recruits know?" I ask, leaning forward. "Do they know that they gave you permission to witness their deaths?" My eyes settled on Jennet. "Do *you* know?"

She nods. "I do."

And that's all she says. It's maddening. She must have lost her mind. Somehow even more than I've lost mine. Finally, I settle back in my chair and huff. "Well, you obviously don't believe that you'll die then."

"I'm not naïve, but I've got to try," she shoots back.

"That's why we need you, Rahym," Nakir says. "You used to work at the Darvaza mines. You know the Door to Hell better than anyone else alive."

"You keep throwing the word 'alive' around like it's going to make me believe that this isn't dangerous," I tell him. "But there's a reason I know it better than anyone else 'alive.' It's because everyone *else* who knew the Door to Hell is dead now."

Well, at least he remembers your first career. Bet you don't know his.

He was an angel, I firmly tell myself. That was his first career.

Still, it's nice.

It's because he needs something from me, that's all.

I didn't always manage a Lodge. That was, after all, Maysa's dream. Before that, I was a poor, stupid young man trying to make some money off the natural gas riches of the Darvaza mine. And before that, as a child, I had my eyes set on one person that I wanted to impress and make a home with.

Spoiler alert, she's sitting right in front of me. Right now.

And she disappeared without warning. But that ended up being a blessing in disguise. Because that's when Maysa and I got close. That's when I fell in love with my future wife and put all of my energy into a dowry so her father would give his blessing.

And I wouldn't have traded that for all of the natural gas in all the world.

My mind has blocked a lot of those memories, of the time when I put my life at risk every day. The mine was the most dangerous job imaginable, mainly because you went *into* the Door to Hell to do your damn job. I personally have stepped through that threshold more times than I care to count. Braving uncontrollable fires, demonlings, and even worse.

All in the name of money and dreams.

Miners died all the time. That's a big reason I no longer work there; they shut down the mine because of too many deaths.

Yeah. Seriously crazy stuff. And now Nakir wants me to go back there.

And this time, with no money and in the name of one crazy, insane dream of breaking the curse.

"Yeah," I mutter in agreement.

"Pardon?" Jennet asks.

I shake my head. "Nothing. So you want me to help lead you into the Door to Hell—again—because you suddenly think it will work this time?"

Nakir leans forward. "Yes. Because at the other side of the Door is the Watchtower. And that's where we'll kill Abaddon."

I blink and throw my head back and laugh. "Oh my God, you must have that memorized!" I say, clutching at my belly. "I think that's the same bullshit you spewed to me all those years ago when we created the Halos. I think it was word for word."

Abaddon is the Demon Lord who oversees the Door to

Hell. It's because of him that we're cursed. And if we kill him, we can live normal lives.

Nakir spouted that nonsense to anyone who would listen.

His face doesn't betray any expression. "The dream has remained the same."

"Let me tell you how it will go, 'old friend,'" I say, leaning forward. "I know you have this big beef with Abbadon. That the curse will just magically disappear as soon as Abbadon does. And we won't have to worry about ever running out of energy again."

Well, except to sleep.

"Honestly, if I didn't have to worry about Hibernation, I don't think I'd ever sleep again," I continue. I think Nakir and Jennet are not following me, but I continue anyway. "So we know *how* you kill Abbadon. You still have your stabby thingy?"

Nakir doesn't move a muscle. "The Sword of Jan? Yes."

The Sword of Jan, the symbol of souls and vitality, bestowed to Nakir by God Himself before Nakir fell. It was meant to be a beacon of hope for mankind. In some ways, it still is, as it's theoretically the only way to kill Abaddon.

So Nakir says.

"Good," I say with a curt nod. "Now you just have to fly to the Watchtower to do the deed. Because," and I point at him to emphasize my point, "you're saying that I know the Door to Hell better than anyone. Well, let me tell you that there's at least forty miles of uncontrollable Hell between here and the Watchtower. It's all desert. No water. No food. Nothing more than maybe some bugs you can eat, I guess, if you get hungry enough. I can recommend a few beetles to you."

Nakir seems prepared for this. "We have plenty of supplies for the journey."

"Bravo," I say sarcastically, clapping slowly. Expending energy, but I'm on a roll. "But that doesn't say anything about the demonlings that reside there. That will kill you as soon as the Hibernation takes over. And it *will* take you over. There's no getting across the desert without expending *everything*. And," I say, leaning back, smacking my forehead, "I forgot the fires! They killed everyone in my mining unit! Everyone I worked with, because yes, we know they work in a pattern. But they don't like to follow convention, oh no. Because just when you think you know how they work, the wind changes and the wildfires spread, and you die."

"You know where the Door Stops are," Jennet adds defensively.

I chuckle bitterly. "Yes, how could I forget about those! Have you ever seen a Door Stop, Jennet? They make them sound like a place where you can call 'Sanctuary!' and you can sleep to your heart's content. Maybe even make a pot of Zelenyi Chai tea."

Jennet's cheeks flush, but I can't stop myself from running my mouth.

For a guy who tries to conserve energy, you sure do ramble a lot.

"You know what they are?" I ask. "Rocky outcroppings. Basically, just parts in the desert that have a little bit of shade and block the wind. Sometimes they're caves, and sometimes, they're just rocks, but you don't know until that's your only choice. And, yes, when I worked in the mines, they were where we stopped to catch our breath. And most of *those* people died. And the farther into the Door you go, the more sand and death you find and the fewer Door Stops there are. Get the picture?"

"I do," Jennet says.

But she doesn't budge. I don't know why she isn't budg-

ERIN HAYES & REBECCA HAMILTON

ing. Because I've basically just painted a sign with the word "DANGER" on it, and she's just ignoring it.

But Nakir knows better. Hell, he *should* know better. Maybe he's lost his mind as much as me these days.

"What's the farthest you've ever gone into the Door?" Nakir asks.

What the hell is he thinking?

"Ten, eleven miles, I suppose. Why?" When he doesn't answer, I press the question harder. "That took careful planning and two days to do it and live to come back home. Because this whole four-hour curse means it's too dangerous to go any farther than that. So again—*why* do you ask?"

"I mentioned that we had a secret weapon," Nakir says.

"Yeah, you did," I say. "Your stabby thingy doesn't count, mainly because you had that last time."

He rolls his eyes. "That is not what I mean."

I bristle. "So tell me."

"Again, *her.*"

I see Jennet's cheeks are colored slightly. "What does *she* have to do with it?"

"*She* has a very special ability," Jennet cuts in, obviously annoyed that we're talking about her as if she's not there.

I watch Jennet as she straightens up. "You didn't know this about me..." she says. "When we were kids, Rahym..." Her voice trails off, embarrassed.

I stare at her. "What?"

"That I could do things. Like this." She holds out her hand, and I see the purple glow of *power* in her palm, pulsating in an unnatural ethereal light.

My immediate reaction is a yelp, followed by a curse word as I scoot as far away from her as my chair allows me to.

Not far enough. Nowhere near far enough.

28

"Y—y—you can do magic?" I ask in both awe and terror. "Th—th—then that makes you—"

"A witch?" she says with a nod. "That was why I suddenly disappeared after my father died. I went to go train with my kind." She gestures with her thumb to a trio behind her. They look nothing like the witches from my imagination.

"And now you're back," I say. "Why? What brought you back?"

"Because," Jennet says quietly, "I'm the only one who can do this."

And before I can stop her, she reaches out to me, and her hand falls on my leg. I nearly leap out of my skin at the touch, but then a warm, calming sensation thrills through me. And the place where she is touching me suddenly feels very much alive. Like, refreshed and ready to take the world on. It's as if the energy I've been conserving within myself is replenished.

And...

She takes her hand off and inhales, her breath shuddering slightly. "I've just extended your energy by about thirty minutes," she says. Meanwhile, though, her voice is strained.

Nakir's expression is soft as he watches her.

Concern?

Nah, the only person Nakir ever feels concern for is himself.

"It takes away the same amount of energy from me, though," Jennet adds quietly. She sighs and sits back in her chair, the headrest and armrests supporting her.

Nakir takes over the conversation then. "So you see how she's our secret weapon."

I shake my head. "No. No, I really don't."

"No?" The angel leans forward. "She can help us prolong

our energy. We're no longer limited by what the curse gives us. We now have more time."

"It looks like it limits her," I say, nodding in Jennet's direction. She doesn't answer, doesn't move. And that affirms my thoughts more than anything else. "You can't expect to make it all the way to the Watchtower simply because Jennet can make you feel powerful for eight hours a day."

"No," Nakir says. "But that's why we have three other witches with us. No other one can do Jennet's trick, but they each have their own special power that can help us. Plus, there are four other humans like yourself who *can make a difference.*"

"So you've got your whole team of Halos again," I say.

Nakir nods. "We just need our guide. *You.*"

"You can't think that this will actually work."

"I'm an angel of God, Rahym. I've been to Heaven. I love Earth and all you crazy humans. I know that what we're going through is worse than Hell right now. And I will do everything within my power to fix it."

"Well, good luck," I tell him. "You've been wrong about everything you said."

He leans back, eyebrows raising. "How do you mean?"

"You said that if I heard you out, it would change my mind and I would join you on this crazy adventure." I smile sadly and shake my head. "I'm sorry, but that ain't happening."

Nakir's expression changes from disbelief to outright disappointment. He crosses his arms. "So that's how it's going to be?"

I get up from my seat. "Yes. That's how it's going to be. I'll give you and your group another night here because I can tell you've spent way too much energy trying to persuade me.

Especially her." I wave distractedly at Jennet. She glowers at me.

"Where are you going now?" Nakir asks as I pass him.

"I'm going to complete number nineteen on my to-do list," I say, bristling. "I need to purge everything from my life that reminds me too much of the past." *Including him.*

"What was it all for, then?" he yells as I stride out the door. "You tried it once!"

I look back at him, feeling something akin to fury rise in me.

He has no idea what it's like being a human, does he?

He may not have his wings right now. He may even look slightly more human without them. But he definitely doesn't understand.

So I tell him. "That was when I had something to die for. And that something died before me."

Nakir's face softens. "I've spent the last three years regretting that day. I'm sorry."

"Nowhere near as much as I am."

CHAPTER 5

A nother whack to make a noticeable difference.
At least that's what I tell myself.

So I swing the hatchet once more, and while bits of charred bark and charcoal break off in brittle slivers, I can't tell that I'm doing much to the charred tree. It's been about a half-hour since I stepped outside, and the sun is beating down on me as I try to take down this forsaken tree.

Nothing. Big surprise there.

"Shut up," I mutter.

Really, what are you doing with your time? You tried and you're going to kill yourself trying to remove this tree.

"No, I won't."

Yes, you will.

"I said shut up!" I yell, slamming the hatchet into the trunk of the tree. It wedges itself in there with a hollow thud, and I feel the tears prick my eyes.

Goddammit, I'm a grown man crying. Over a goddamn tree.

"Who are you talking to?" a voice rings out.

I turn at the sound, immediately recognizing it, although I don't want to talk to *her*. It's easy to be mad at Nakir, because he should know better. But it's Jennet who's talking to me right now. And I know that she is following the angel to her death.

"No one," I tell her. "I'm not talking to anyone."

Jennet watches me for a few moments more as I try to ignore her again. Unfortunately, that seems impossible, because she's there in the back of my mind. I can't stop thinking about what Nakir said. I can't stop thinking about what she is.

"Is that the tree?" she asks softly.

It's a question that makes me grunt as I try to remove the hatchet, unsure what to do next. The fight has left me, and I grip the handle tightly. It doesn't budge, and I close my eyes and sigh.

"Yes."

This is Maysa's tree. The one that she planted when we were just children. All three of us. We grew up in Derweze, before Maysa's father took over the Lodge from his father. So Maysa moved away, leaving Jennet and me together to grow up in a lonely harsh world. We'd visit her when our families would deliver supplies.

But things always seemed strained after that.

And she planted this giant fig tree that grew in a place where nothing else would.

"See this, Rahym? This is a sign of hope. That despite everything, there is still hope for us to grow here."

That was her voice in my head. Not my own voice. I could never confuse her voice with mine.

She was proud of the tree. Hell, I was proud of her for being proud of it.

33

And now it's burned to a crisp. Something else I couldn't protect.

"She always was a kind soul," Jennet says quietly.

I don't answer her, but the muscles in my jaw keep clenching and unclenching. I've been fighting off the despair for so long, and now Jennet is inviting it back into our lives.

You have a fallen angel in your Lodge, but she is being the Devil.

Oh, my brain is so clever when it wants to be. I huff angrily and put my hands on my hips. Jennet has a small, sad smile on her face as she looks the tree up and down. Her mouth is slightly parted as she does so, taking her time as she looks at it. Finally, those blue, blue eyes focus back on me. And they're sad.

So sad.

"What happened to it?" she asks.

My throat tightens. "Wildfire. Nearly burned the Lodge down. And it..." My chest constricts against the words, because it seems like every time I say it out loud, it just drives that nail further into my soul.

No wonder I talk to myself so much.

You're so aware of that, too.

"...did that fire kill Maysa?" Jennet asks, her voice tiny.

"And Beste," I add. "Our daughter."

There is no answer. Jennet knows without asking what Beste meant to me, even though I try to bury her as far as possible.

"I'm so sorry," she finally whispers.

I nod vigorously. Too vigorously, but at least it gives my head something to do. "Yeah," I say. "And that's exactly why I don't want you doing this with Nakir. He's going to get you killed."

"Most likely."

I stare at her, open-mouthed. "And that doesn't bother you?"

She shrugs. "I'm a witch, Rahym. I've always been shunned by humans and...*other beings* alike. I know it's a long shot for me to actually help on this crazy thing." She laughs and places a strand of hair behind her ear. "But if there's even one slim chance, then I'm going to do it."

"Why?"

"Because we all deserve a chance to be happy."

"I can't," I tell her helplessly. "I can't do that."

She nods. "Nakir thought that talking with you would change your mind." She smirks. "I knew better. I didn't expect you to come with us."

I blink.

Well, she sure has you pegged.

It feels like my soul is bared for the entire world to see. "So why did you come here, then?"

Jennet considers her answer. "Well, to tell you the truth, I really just wanted to see you. It's been a long time, Rahym."

I don't say anything to that. How can you when you haven't seen the person in decades? She risked coming here to see me? When Nakir is leading them to their deaths?

She keeps watching me, though, and I still have that strange, transparent feel to my body, like she can see all of my muscles, tendons, even my very own thoughts.

Which are not very safe.

"I just wanted to see you," she repeats softly.

I stiffen. "Do you really think you have a chance?" I ask, changing the subject. I don't know how to address what she said. Or process any of it.

She seems to know this, too, and goes along with my change in subject.

"Even just the slightest chance makes it all worth it." She

licks her full lips. "I know you made the ultimate sacrifice in the past to do this. I know it was cruel to ask you to try again, and I'm sorry for that." Her face softens. "But I'm glad I got to see you. Even if it was for the last time."

She turns to head back into the Lodge. "You should probably come in soon," she says, nodding at the hatchet. "I may have given you an extra thirty minutes of energy, but it's not even noon yet; if you push yourself too hard, you're going to go into Hibernation out here. And I wouldn't forgive myself if that happened."

Before Jennet disappears in the doorway, I ask, "How did... How did you meet Nakir? Last thing I knew, he hated any witch."

She chuckles lightly. "That's probably why the curse hasn't been broken in fifty years." She winks at me, and I feel something shudder to life within my chest. "You'd be surprised what a witch can do when she sets her mind to it."

Then she's gone. I look back at the hatchet, and, deciding that it is indeed too much effort to take it back to the shed and clean up my mess, leave the damn thing in the tree.

CHAPTER 6

Rahym. *Rahym, wake up!*
I fight my subconscious at first. I feel weak, with the Hibernation just minutes away from grabbing me and collapsing me into oblivion. I know that I've expended too much energy today, and if I wake up and have trouble falling back asleep, I'm going to lose control of my body to the curse.

But there's something that makes me pay attention. A smell lingers in the air. One that chills me all the way to the bone.

Mainly because I recognize what it is.

"Shit!" I yell, springing to my feet, the last vestiges of sleep sloughing off me as panic overtakes me.

Something is burning. And as I take stock of my surroundings, I realize that the Lodge is going up in flames.

"Yusup!" I yell, running out of my personal quarters and heading for the landing on the second floor. "Faruk! We have a situation!"

Do we ever.

ERIN HAYES & REBECCA HAMILTON

I don't answer as I breathe heavily, despite telling myself that I shouldn't inhale the smoke-filled air. The fire is on the bottom floor, licking its way up the rafters to the second floor. I have guests on both floors. Guests who may be sleeping. Or in the throes of their Hibernations.

They're going to die if I don't do something.

"FARUK! YUSUP!"

Moments later, I'm greeted by Faruk, a big man himself, although not as big as Yusup. He's dressed in a pair of trousers, looking as if he has just been jostled from sleep like me.

"Boss?" he asks. He looks down the stairs, fear in his eyes.

"Where's Yusup?" I demand.

"Hibernation," he answers. Worry drips from his voice like amber. He knows how little chance we have of saving everyone without Yusup's help.

I curse under my breath. I shouldn't work my staff this much. Not to the point of them losing control over their bodies like this. I know better.

Take action, Rahym. Berate yourself later.

Deal with the consequences later.

"Get the rest of the staff—those who can get up. Knock on all the doors on the second floor and *get our guests out of here!*"

Maysa always wanted to protect and save weary travelers. And I realize with rising dread that I'm not going to be able to protect all of them.

Faruk nods without further comment and gets to work, ticking off the first item on my short to-do list that I gave him. Good man.

I run downstairs, ready to deal with the truly exhausted, those who couldn't make it up the stairs.

38

To my surprise, Nakir intercepts me at the base of the stairs. "Evacuation?" he asks.

"Yes." I glare at him, as if he's the cause of all this. And, most likely, he is. I saw the demonlings' cloud of dust rising earlier today when there hadn't been any sort of activity from them for weeks. The coincidence was too much. Why the fuck didn't I do something to stop it?

More to the point, why didn't I send Nakir packing when he showed up last night?

Because you have a soft spot for Jennet?

And Nakir probably knew that. Well played, asshole. Now I'll have to play well myself in order to save all of us.

"Get your crew out of here," I tell him. "And watch out for demonlings!"

Nakir doesn't nod and doesn't say anything. He's on his feet, gathering up the small band of people that he brought with him. Some stir awake.

Some don't.

Goddammit. Some of them have already fallen into Hibernation.

Nakir grabs them anyway, hefting them over his shoulders like sacks of potatoes. I glance back up the stairs, concerned as I haven't seen Yusup or Faruk or the others. I have six other guests who were staying here, innocent bystanders to the destruction that Nakir brought with him.

I should have known.

Save it.

As if to punctuate my subconscious, I hear the splintering crack of a support beam as fire eats away at it. The upstairs won't last much longer. And if we're in here when the building collapses...

"FARUK!" I leap over the counter and grab my yataghan. The Lodge being on fire isn't the only thing that

I'm worried about. I'm more concerned about the ugly moth-erfuckers that want to greet us out front. That's the only reason they'd set fire to my Lodge.

I know that when buildings caught fire in the old days, there were ways of putting it out. In fact, there were so-called "fire-men" who would rush in to douse the flames with water. With the advent of the curse, we no longer have the luxury of saving anything but our own asses.

If we're lucky.

"FARUK!" I roar again.

"Move, human!"

I don't recognize the voice—a young, female voice that is higher pitched and more lilting than Jennet's.

But I learned long ago not to question who's ordering, only to heed *what* they're ordering, and I oblige without hesitation.

I swivel and duck to see Jennet standing in the middle of the great room, flanked by three of the Halos that she came in with. Her hand is on an older woman, and I see the purple glow of power seeping into the older woman's exposed arms. Jennet's eyes are closed, as if she's in deep concentration.

And the elderly woman, with her white hair pulled back into a knot at the nape of her neck, is glaring up at the fire eating up the staircase. Her eyes shimmer with unnatural power as well.

I realize what she is. And a quick glance at the other two people with Jennet confirm what they are as well.

Witches.

One's a short, thin man, and the other is a young woman, probably still in her teens. She's shooting daggers at me with her eyes, confirming that she's the one who yelled at me to move. She motions with her arm for me to stand next to them.

In a building that's burning down, the safest place is probably next to the witches.

True.

I hurry to them, and they include me in their circle. It certainly doesn't *feel* safer here.

"The fire," the older woman says through gritted teeth. "There's too much."

She must have thought she could control it, which makes me wonder if she has elemental abilities over fire. If she's a fire elemental, she should be able to weave and bend the fire at will. If she can't, that doesn't give me much hope we'll survive.

Jennet takes in a shuddering breath. Fascinated, I watch as she pushes a surge of purple power into the older woman's body. "*Try again.*"

The older woman nods, her eyes never leaving the all-consuming fire. "I…" she says. "I can't—"

But she's not the one who passes out. Jennet gasps as her knees buckle, and the rest of her falls like a house of cards as the Hibernation takes control of her body. She spent herself in helping the older woman, and she's now paying the price.

I'm too slow to catch her, but the man next to me does. He grunts as he takes the weight of her body.

"Jennet!" the girl cries.

"I've got her," the man says, straining under Jennet's slight weight.

The older woman breathes heavily, the glisten of sweat on her cheeks. "I can't save us," she whispers. "We have to leave. *Now.*"

The man next to me grunts. "Let's go."

I look up to see Nakir carrying four people over his shoulders and one in his arms. Several others are with them,

41

conscious, and with Faruk dragging Yusup's big body, I let out a sigh of relief that everyone is accounted for.

You haven't let down Maysa yet.

"Yet," I mumble. My eyes focus on Nakir, and that propels my brain forward. "We can't leave. Not with those things out there."

Nakir gives me a cool look. "Then what do you suggest we do?"

I open my mouth, but I'm cut off by the loud groaning of support beams weakening.

We're going to die if we don't get out of here.

We're going to die if we go out there anyway.

The girl next to me closes her eyes and hums lightly as her hair moves as if it's floating in the breeze. She concentrates for a long moment, then opens her eyes.

"There are seven demonlings out there," she says determinedly. More magic, this time in the form of sensing where the demonlings are. Who are these people that Nakir found? "Four out front and three in the back." Her eyes snap open, and she proudly lifts her chin as she talks to Nakir. "If we go out both doors at once, we'll catch them off guard."

She's insane. I don't even know if the back door is unblocked.

Nakir, meanwhile, takes this in stride. "Right. Rahym, you lead Sena, Kerem, and Nury through the back since you know your Lodge. I'll face the others out front."

I want to protest, but he passes by me, and I see the scabbard strapped to his back. He still has that Godforsaken Sword of Jan strapped on. Five feet of Damascus steel and a bone handle, it takes inhuman strength to wield the weapon.

The sword can slice through the fabric of time and space —that's another thing he's told me, but I don't doubt that if he's greeted by demonlings in the front, he'll have no trouble dispatching them.

Meanwhile, my group will be slaughtered. I look to the three that I'm with—Sena the elderly woman, Kerem the wiry man carrying Jennet, and the man who passed out when the Halos arrived last night—and I wonder what the hell they could do to stop demonlings from killing us.

Nothing.

The yataghan in my hand feels slippery from sweat. The heat is building in here now, and it's either we leave now and die at the hands of the demonlings or we die inside the Lodge.

"It's never easy," I mutter under my breath.

Nakir gets a wide grin as he regards me. "That's the spirit, Rahym."

He rushes toward the entrance. I swallow, feeling the lump at my throat bob up and down in nervousness as I look to my small group. They wait for my answer, as if I'm supposed to lead them. I can't help feeling like I've turned into Nakir and I'm now leading them to their deaths.

"This way."

They follow me out the back like shadows. I keep glancing behind me to make sure that Jennet is still with us, that Kerem hasn't discarded her in favor of faster travel.

He's carrying her like a lamb across his shoulders.

To my immense relief, the back door to the Lodge, where one leaves to use the outhouse, isn't blocked by fire or any fallen beams. But as we walk toward it, the hallway collapses behind us.

The older woman looks back at the timbers and bricks now blocking us from any alternative route. "Looks like this is our only way out now." Her mood is almost detached, as if she's watching this happen to someone else.

Meanwhile, I'm trying not to let my eyes bulge out of their sockets.

"Too bad Fatma's not with us to see if the demonlings are still here," Nury says. The cheeks of the young man burn intensely at that comment. Kerem shares a knowing smile with the old woman, and I'm so goddamn tired of pseudo-heroics from these people.

"How good are you with that yataghan, miner?" the old woman asks.

"Decent." I grip it harder. "But it won't help if there are too many demonlings."

That knowing smile from the old woman widens. "Just trust me to keep the flames at bay."

I want to tell her that, no, I don't trust her one bit. In the short time I've known her, she's failed to gain my trust one hundred percent of the time.

But what choice do you have right now?

"And I've got your back," the young man—Nury—says, unsheathing a small dagger. It gives me a little more confidence, but small daggers, yataghans, and bravado won't save us. A miracle will.

Here goes nothing.

I throw the door open out to the cold desert air of the night. Out here, a breeze blows that smells slightly of the ash from the Door. There's something else; something pungent and rank hits my nose and threatens to choke me.

I see why.

Those bastard demonlings even set fire to the shithouse with their torches. No wonder I'm choking, although it seems like a smart tactic as my eyes are watering so badly right now, I can't see.

Some fighter I am.

And then I'm attacked by a demonling that launches

itself from the roof of the back patio. It lands on me, its claws raking across my back as it looks for purchase in my flesh. I feel my night clothes immediately soak from blood.

I roar, straightening as I fling it off me, hacking away with my yataghan. It catches the demonling by surprise, grazing its upper bicep with the blade of my knife. Illuminated by the fires, I can see it literally licking its wounds as it glares at me.

"I forgot how ugly you assholes are."

The word *demonling* makes them sound like little gremlins, but they stand just shy of an average man's height with thick, rubbery, rust-red skin. This one has a pair of horns curling from just above its brow line, and it has a bad underbite, its lower teeth protruding in haphazard brick shapes. There is a tuft of black hair on its ugly head, and its yellow eyes watch me as it snarls. Its tail whips about like a pissed-off cat.

I need to do more than piss it off.

And this is just one. There are two others, and I have no idea where they might be hiding.

Inhuman screams from the front of the Lodge distract both of us. It takes me a moment to realize what happened, but as it cuts off shortly, another scream rents the night, and it clicks into place. Nakir is taking care of the demonlings out front. Well, good for him. That does nothing to help me back here.

Meanwhile, things do not go well with the demonling in front of me.

The thing rears back and screeches at me, spittle flying in my face, with breath that matches the horrid odor from the burning shithouse.

I respond by kicking it in the face—anything to shut that maw.

Another weight lands on my back, and I stagger, too overwhelmed to deal with the growling beast in front of me and its companion now on my back. I flail, trying to dislodge it, but I can't take my eyes off the first demonling because if I do, it'll attack me. They're sneaky like that.

"Some help!" I shout to my group.

At first, I don't see anything, but then Nury tears the thing off my back and, with lightning-quick motions, slits the demonling's throat. The beast splutters as black blood spews from the wound.

One down.

Did not expect that kind of attack out of the embarrassed young man. Apparently, he's good with a blade. I make a mental note not to piss him off if we make it through this alive.

I want to say thanks, but we don't have time, and I don't want to distract him.

"Behind you!" Sena shouts.

I turn, a moment too late, to see a thrown torch hurtling toward me. The inferno reaches out, ready to take me as I hear the rumbling laughter of the demonling behind it.

The fire stops, as if it hit a glass wall, unable to pass through it. This surprises both the demonling and me.

"Move, Rahym!" the old woman shouts, a strain to her voice.

She's doing something to the fire.

I don't dare question it. I sprint, catching the demonling in the chest with a hack of my yataghan. It screeches, clutching at the gaping wound, and I kick it to the ground. The young man at my side slices through the demonling's neck, and its head flies to land in the sand, blood steaming in the night.

Two down.

Never thought we'd make it this far. But still…

"Where's the other one?" I demand. I whirl, looking around us, to see if I can spot it.

Then I do, as it catches me in the side, its claws tearing into the flesh just below my ribcage. The agony tears through me, and I scream.

This demonling is smaller than the other two, but its laughter is deeper. It knows what it's doing to me, how much it hurts, and it's enjoying it.

It's all too much.

I don't know what comes over me. Something ugly. Something feral that won't be sated until the beast that is impaling me is dead. It's the same feral thing that made me not kill myself in the despair after my wife's and daughter's deaths.

It's survival. And I bend it to my will, grabbing my yataghan as I spear the demonling in the eye. It falls to the ground, dying, but I'm not done with it yet. I proceed to hack away at it while the hot, black blood lands on me and spills out around me.

I go berserk.

I hack and I hack and I hack, wanting to kill it, wipe it away from this world. It and things like it have caused so much pain and torment, it's all I can do to not rip off its skin.

This is what killed my family. This is what burned my Lodge to the ground. This is why the curse weighs so heavily on us. If I could just kill all of them, then I could sleep easier at night.

I make a decision, one that is unexpected for me, but it's one that I know there's no coming back from.

I realize that my hearing was gone at some point, because I suddenly hear someone shouting my name, over and over again, trying to stop me from overexerting myself.

"—*hym! RAHYM!*"

I look up to see Nakir and the rest of the group that went

out of the front door staring at me in both disgust and disbe-lief. Nakir's face is set into a stone-like visage as his eyes flick to the now-mound of flesh at my feet and then back at me. He has an expression of wonder and fear on his face.

The others, from Faruk to Sena and Yusup—both workers that I've known for years and Halos that I've only just met—watch me with that same expression.

I grit my teeth, knowing that I must look like something back from the dead, covered in the gore of this beast.

And then a combination of the Hibernation and my injury grabs at my body.

No one's close enough to catch me, even if they wanted to.

CHAPTER 7

I still have nightmares, even while I'm in the throes of the Hibernation.

They all go the same way.

Flames eating at me. Burning my side. I feel my side hurting where I had talons pierce me, intending to kill.

I hear screams, screams I can't get to in time, before my body seizes underneath me and I fall hard to the earth, my own blood spilling out in front of me. I hear their voices echo again and again in my mind, ricocheting inside my skull and shattering every piece of my soul.

Screams. Maysa screaming, Beste screaming.

I can't do anything to save them.

I lay on the dirt, unable to move, unable to reach them. All I can do is witness their deaths with my ears.

I want to wake up. Get up from my spot and save them.

Why can't I save them?

Why am I so useless?

Why am I cursed?

I must get. Up. NOW.

I scream, kicking aside the furs on top of me. Ready to bolt. Rage has settled in over me, clouding my eyesight. I just have to get out of here to save them. I'm awake, my limbs can move, and I can still save my family.

"Rahym!"

That voice.

The rage ebbs from my vision, and I find myself staring right into Jennet's turquoise eyes. Her hair is disheveled, and while she's not afraid of me, she watches me with the wariness one would have around a sleeping rabid dog.

The rabid dog being me.

I let go of her, realizing that I've been clutching her roughly by the shoulders, probably enough to hurt her.

"Sorry," I mutter, combing a hand through my hair. "I'm sorry, Jennet."

Her fingers lightly caress my bicep. "It's all right. Some have violent fits when they come out of Hibernation."

I sigh. "No excuse."

"After everything you've been through, Rahym," she says, and I can hear the somber smile in her voice, "no one faults you for what happened."

That makes me look up at her and take further stock of my surroundings.

With a sinking feeling, I see that I'm not in my Lodge. The burlap panels of a tent surround us, fluttering in the wind. It's daytime, meaning that I've been out for quite some time. I feel somewhat relieved to be alive.

At the same time, I know why I'm in a tent, sleeping on a sand floor, and a strangled noise escapes my throat.

A look of anguish crosses Jennet's face before she masks it with a deep sigh. "Demonlings attacked last night. They—"

"The Lodge?"

She licks her lips, and her eyes are listless.

That's all the information I need.

"No..." I whisper, shaking my head. "*No.*"

"Rahym..." she starts. She reaches for me, but I roll to my feet and storm out of the makeshift tent to go out into the bright daylight of the desert. I have to see it for myself. I know we can't be far, not after the events of last night.

I freeze to my spot just outside. We're not far at all from where the Lodge used to be.

I see the still-smoldering, burning embers of the place that I called home. A dream that I shared with Maysa and our daughter.

It's gone, reduced to...*this*...

"Rahym!" Jennet cries, following me out of the tent. She stops, seeing my reaction, as if she's almost afraid of the repercussions. Gingerly, she reaches out to put a hand on my arm, but I shy away from it. "Rahym, I'm so sorry," she whispers.

I don't even look at her. I can't take my eyes off it.

Maysa. What would Maysa think?

She'd have killed me for letting this happen.

Suddenly, something ripples up from the depths of my soul, growing in crescendo as it hits my throat. A low laugh escapes my throat as the remnants of my sanity crack. I laugh, throwing my head back with it. Once it starts, I can't stop. Jennet's face is fearful as my features morph into that of a gremlin.

I'm laughing at the absurdity of it all.

What's the point? Of this, of anything else, if it's just going to be stripped from us?

My to-do list would never get done now. The tree is now

gone, and number nineteen is now struck through. I wasn't even the one to tear it down, and I lost everything else with it.

I'll never get that closure. I'll never get to put that final stone on the gravemarker of my soul.

I collapse to my knees, laughing until tears stream down my face. And I keep going even beyond that.

CHAPTER 8

"I'll do it."

Nakir's hand shoveling bread to his mouth stops midway between mouthfuls as he snaps his head to me, astonished. "Are you sure?"

Great. Blurting that suddenly during breakfast doesn't make you look any less crazy after having a nervous breakdown in the desert.

But I just did. And I mean every word of it.

I nod in answer to Nakir's question. "I am. I'll help you goons on this crazy-ass quest."

We're sitting around in a loose circle inside one of the tents. Yusup, Faruk and my staff all look shell-shocked after last night's events—probably even as much as I do—but at least they're alive. The Halos manage to look relieved.

All except Jennet.

Her expression is hard, intense, like she's trying to read into why I've made my decision. I want to take her aside and tell her that there's nothing left of me. That I'm nothing without my Lodge. I'm nothing without Maysa.

"You know that you could very well die, right?" she asks pointedly.

She sounds a lot like you did.

I shrug. "Life ain't going to get any better this way. I might as well do something." *Not to mention that my soul has already died.*

"Rahym—" Jennet starts.

"He's made up his mind," Nakir cuts in, his voice harsh. But Jennet turns on him, her eyes flashing angrily.

"He's obviously making this choice out of grief," she says, motioning toward me.

"Grief sometimes makes our choices for us," he says.

She fumes angrily. "Yes, but he's not in his right mind, Nakir, and that could get us all killed if he loses it at the wrong time."

"I'm still here. You realize that, right?" I ask mildly as I place my own piece of bread in my mouth. But they're too embroiled in their argument to even consider my remark.

"We've all lost someone," Nakir tells her. "That's why any of us are here. To make a better future for those who still have hope."

"We shouldn't take advantage of someone right after they've lost everything," she shoots back.

"Again, I'm still here," I point out. "And thanks for the reminder."

"Rahym has been through enough to know what's driving us." Nakir leans in to Jennet, his eyes imploring her to agree. "He's our only shot of making it through the Door."

This stops Jennet's protests, and she sits back, chewing on her thumbnail. Things never change. I remember her doing that when we were kids, a nervous tick of hers when something never sat well with her. Growing up in the desert next to the Door, a lot of things never sat well with us.

"If it helps any," the young witch says to all of us, breaking into the conversation. She's the one who sensed the demonlings outside of the Lodge last night. "I'd like to point out that most of our supplies were destroyed last night, so we still have to go back to Derweze to pick up more. That should give Rahym some time to reconsider his agreement before we go into the Door."

Nakir gives the girl a broad smile. "And that's why you're one of the best witches out there, Fatma," he says in a fatherly tone.

She blushes at his appreciation.

Jennet considers this. "What do you think, Rahym?" she asks, her eyes flicking back to me. She wants me to say no, to save my life, because she thinks I can't make a rational decision at this point.

With our energy limitations, Derweze would be an extra day of travel. That would be plenty of time for me to change my mind. Not that I would change my mind. I tend to be stubborn that way. My tenacity at getting things done around the Lodge is testament to that.

"Sounds good," I say through dry lips.

Jennet glowers at me as she turns back to her food.

I don't blame her.

I'm not a very smart man. Never have been. And this is the latest example of my genius.

Which reminds me, I don't want more people to get killed on behalf of my foolishness.

"Actually," I say cautiously, "I will travel with you on one condition."

And Nakir wasn't going to be a fan of it.

CHAPTER 9

"No, boss," Yusup says.

The big man is in tears. I don't judge, because I've had my own tears myself through the years, but it really doesn't suit him. His big cheekbones act as walls, meaning that the rivulets have to go nearly all the way to his ears before gravity takes them down his face.

Good thing he doesn't cry all too often, then.

I hide my smirk, which is fighting to shine through my seriousness. He's allowed to do what he wants. After all, good-byes are never easy.

I know that better than anyone.

Faruk is near tears himself as is the rest of my staff, but Yusup is the only one to openly cry. I have seven employees to worry about: Yusup, Faruk, Hamza, and Damla are my security staff, working in shifts to keep my travelers safe, while Beyza, Tuana, and Deniz work to keep the place in order from turning over beds to cooking warm meals.

They all did that. Past tense. Your Lodge is no more.

I clench my jaw at my inner voice, telling it to shut up,

because I don't want to join Yusup in crying in front of every-one. I don't want the rest of my staff crying, because that takes energy.

"You will be fine," I tell Yusup, giving him a brotherly pat on the back. His muscles feel like solid brick. *Damn, he's strong.* I'm going to miss him on the road through the Door to Hell. "We all knew this day was coming eventually."

Even if they hadn't considered it, I knew it was coming. In our world, nothing is forever. Everything is taken from us. To make peace with that now is to guard your heart before it crumbles.

"But why should we go to Merv without you?" Hamza asks, his deep voice a rumble.

I nod conspiratorially toward Nakir and the other Halos as they pack up their camp. "Trust me, you don't want to be anywhere near these guys. You think last night was bad? They're going to bring death and destruction wherever they go. Like moths to flame, you can bet your ass there will be demonlings following us." I nod to the small group of shell-shocked travelers that are waiting for their escort to Merv. "Plus, we have our guests to help cross the desert safely. And what's our number one rule?"

"Do everything we can to help our guests," a few mumble in answer. It's something I say a lot, and they repeat with the practiced diligence of children reciting a prayer.

I nod proudly at them, and I know, in my gut, that they'll make it there fine. Damn, I'm going to miss them.

"But what about you?" Faruk asks.

I shrug. "It's not about me anymore."

Tuana clamps a hand to her mouth, stifling a cry. "You were one of the best bosses we've ever had," she tells me.

"Aw, come now, Tuana," I tell her, giving her a sympa-thetic pat. "I've been your only boss."

Granted, I think I have been a good boss, if I do say so myself. While I can be a hardass to my employees, I paid them well and always made sure that they were well-rested in light of the curse. Maysa taught me a lot of things in my time, and patience and humility were her specialty. It's made me a better manager of my staff. It's made me a better man.

Beyza can't take anymore and gives me a hug. "Are you sure you don't want to come with us?" she sobs into my shoulder.

I smile, feeling that strange tightening in my chest which means that my emotions are getting out of control. I swallow back the lump in my throat.

"I'm sure," I say. "I *have* to do this."

I started this quest years ago. Now I'll either finish it or it will finish me. Why am I fighting? I don't really know, except that it's the right thing to do.

Plus, I'd love to stab a few more demonlings through the eyes. God, I hate those bastards.

One of the three horses that I bartered for with Nakir huffs impatiently. "Easy, boy. You'll have your time to shine," I tell the animal. Tuana hiccups a laugh. I'll take that as a victory.

"Will we ever see you again?" Yusup asks, and the rest of my former staff nod.

I stifle the urge to laugh, since it's an absurd question, especially given my mission. There's no coming back from this. So instead, I ask truthfully, "Now why would you want to do that?"

That makes a few snort with bittersweet laughter, a few more tears fall. Time is running short and energy is running even shorter, so we spend a few more minutes hugging and saying good-bye before they head over to the group of travelers with the horses and leave.

I stand stoically, watching them. I don't have the energy to feel remorseful for what I've done, don't have the energy to feel too much of anything right now, and my sarcastic inner voice is gone. So I just watch them, trying to untense my body the entire time.

Wasted energy.

"I know that was hard," a voice says beside me. "They were family to you, weren't they?"

Jennet. Without turning, I close my eyes, sensing her presence near me. I know that she's close enough that I could reach out and take her hand in mine.

But why would I do that?

Then, to my utter surprise, she takes *mine* in hers. It's much smaller than mine, with a delicate touch that only a woman would have. And we stand there like that until Nakir calls for us to leave, heading the opposite direction toward Derweze.

I startle at the sound of his voice and drop her hand. She watches me curiously, her blue eyes imploring me.

"You don't have to do this," she whispers. "You've already given so much, Rahym."

I look out over the dune where I know Yusup and Faruk and all the others are making the trek north to Merv. They're counting on me to help break the curse in any small way I can. Even if it's leading a group of rebels to their deaths.

"I have to try," I tell her, my voice raspy. "Maysa would have wanted me to."

Her eyes cast down. "Okay," she whispers with a nod. "Okay." And as I look at her, I feel that thing—whatever it is—shudder to life once again in my chest.

CHAPTER 10

I have a very different kind of list in my pocket as I stalk up and down the stalls of the bazaar in Derweze.

It goes something like this:

1. *Food (Sena and Kerem)*
2. *Chal (fermented camel's milk) (Fatma)*
3. *Vodka (Fatma)*
4. *Yurts (Murat)*
5. *Horses (Nakir)*
6. *Weapons (Emre)*

And the list goes on and on and on. Far past number nineteen, on a shopping list that one man could never buy for himself in a single day. Like me, Nakir and the Halos lost everything in the fire at the Lodge, and they have to start from scratch in order to get enough supplies for us to travel into the Door. Each member of Halos has certain items that they need to source and find for the entire group. Mine is all the way down the list, for simple navigation through the Door. Like we're going out on a safari or a tour of the Door.

Not that we're trying to save the world or anything.

I take out the note, not because I need reminding of what I'm trying to get, but because I need to keep my hands occupied. Storekeepers peer up at me curiously, as if trying to figure out who I am and what I'm doing.

I guess most people here aren't very lively.

"Maps, compass, binoculars, telescope..." I murmur to myself. All rare treasures in this dilapidated world, especially the binoculars and the telescope. If they haven't been used as spare parts to repair something with glass, then I'm sure they'll cost the same amount as a horse. Or more.

The bazaar is mostly still. Silent. Like a cemetery. Funny, since I remember it being a much livelier place when I was younger. Maybe people had more hope back then. Or maybe I'm seeing everything through the lens of a man who has lost everything.

There's a smattering of fruit carts with decaying produce on them, marked down to nearly free, as it's cheaper to have customers buy the perishable good than it is to deal with it. Tattered fabrics and carpets flutter in the hot, dry breeze, and it seems like only the flies are checking out the bazaar.

That's not entirely true. There are a few customers that flit between shops, but the shopkeepers themselves mostly sit toward the fronts of their establishments, not moving unless there is interest in their wares. Or if there's a thief, which is unlikely, given that they have their more expensive products close at hand.

They're all conserving energy. Smart.

Unlike you.

"Yeah, well, I have stuff to do," I mutter, rubbing my temple.

I spot a map seller at one cart, and he watches me warily as I sort through his maps. I smile crazily at him, giving him the impression that I'm harmless.

Or at least harmless to anyone but myself.

Mostly, these maps are old, torn and faded pieces of paper from the world before, of places I've never heard of or been to. Huge cities and densely packed streets show a time when people could build and build, creating large cities without worrying about the curse.

"Where's this 'New York City' place?" I ask the map seller, holding up one particular map. It looks unlike anywhere I've ever seen, and it's surrounded by seas and water. I can't even imagine.

"Gone," he says with a sniff. "Discounted if you'd like."

Yeah, that won't do me any good, although I'd love to take some energy and study the cartography. I just can't even imagine something like that in all the places I've ever been.

"Do you have one of the Door to Hell?"

The map seller raises his eyebrows in curiosity. "The Door?"

I fight the urge to roll my eyes. "Yes, the Door. I have a death wish, and I really want to find the best place for demonlings to kill me."

His lips press together at my somewhat-joke, and he gets to his feet. He ambles over to a trunk and pulls out a rolled piece of parchment paper. It looks newer than the others and less professional as it's been all hand drawn, but as I smooth it out over other maps, I can recognize a few landmarks including a few Door Stops that I've had the misfortune of spending a terrifying night at.

It's definitely the Door to Hell, although it's crudely drawn, like some miner sat down to remember all the places he'd been. Still, it's better than anything I could draw, especially with a sense of scale, and I can add to it with anything I can remember.

It will work.

I roll it back up. "I'll take this." I wave it.

The map seller curls his lip. "Just take it. Damn thing's cursed anyway."

I give him another wide grin. "Well, thank you kindly, then."

I put it away in my satchel as I move through the bazaar. One thing marked off my list, easier than I expected.

I could get used to that.

The kids of the bazaar don't seem to mind expending energy. I see a boy and a girl chase each other between the stalls, without a care in the world. They'll pass out later into Hibernation, probably the best way for their parents to keep an eye on them, so long as they don't get hurt before then. I cast a furtive glance, trying to locate where their parents are. No one moves to chide the children from hiding underneath tables or squealing at the tops of their lungs.

Are we that afraid that we're no longer playing with our children? I don't remember it being that way with my own daughter. I always made an effort to play with her.

I turn back to them as they rush by me, pure joy on their face. Brother and sister, probably. That same muscle in my chest twists as I watch the girl. She's a little younger than Beste would have been. If Beste had survived...

My eyes catch on something glinting at a booth.

There's a telescope!

For once, I thank my mind for being insistent and over-taking my actions. I loose a breath at the sight of the glass piece of a telescope gleaming in the sun. It's at an old parts shop with loads of scrap metal pieces covering the table.

Hopefully it's still intact. I'm not sure why Nakir thought

it important to have a telescope—after all, the Door to Hell is a wasteland with not much to see—but he insisted that it was important.

So here I am, expending energy, walking up to the cart. The shopkeeper blinks up at me, almost surprised to see that I chose him. Maybe it's my own mannerisms that are making him uneasy.

You make everyone uneasy.

I ignore the sly comment. "How much for the telescope?" I ask, nodding to the piece.

The shopkeeper, a large, rotund man with chubby cheeks—testament to a sedate lifestyle—slides his eyes over to the telescope. "Ten thousand Manat."

"*Ten thousand!*" I spit the words out in disbelief. Not just more than a horse, but more than the price of a legendary Akhal-Teke horse. Ten thousand is more than I've ever seen in my lifetime. I don't have that kind of money.

The shopkeeper only gives a disgruntled nod.

"But why?" Suddenly, I'm wondering if it is as important as Nakir seems to think it is.

"It's a working telescope," the shopkeeper says with a froglike frown. "Not gonna see much of those in the world today."

"But…but…"

You could steal it. There's no way this man would be able to keep up with you. And no one would help him.

That's true. And a stark reminder of the world I live in. I grit my teeth, actually considering it. I'm not a thief, but it's for a good cause. I see the shopkeeper's eyes narrow as he watches me, as if daring me to take it and see what happens. Maybe he has a pistol somewhere.

Maybe you can take the risk.

"Ten thousand Manat isn't too bad for that." Both the

shopkeeper and I twist our heads to look at Jennet smiling as she holds out a wad of cash. "We'll take it."

In the daylight, in this dead bazaar, Jennet is a lily in the desert, foreign, beautiful, and completely out of place. She has a wrap around her head, covering up her dark hair. But her eyes. There's no hiding her supernatural eyes.

She doesn't look at me. Instead, she focuses solely on the shopkeeper. Suspicious, he takes the money from her and, to my surprise, expends the energy to count it, licking his fingers for contact with the paper.

"It's all there," I say, offended.

Jennet and the man don't acknowledge my comment. She has a strange, placating smile on her face, while he completely ignores her and finishes counting.

"Yes, it is," he mutters finally.

He meets my eyes and gives a gruff nod toward the telescope. Not even going to wrap it for me. It's times like this that make me realize how much more hospitality we shared back at the Lodge. That was all Maysa's doing. She wanted our Lodge to be an oasis in the desolation in our world.

But Maysa isn't here.

I feel the lump in my throat bob up and down as I swallow dryly at the thought. My wife isn't here. I'm left in a world that is without her gentle grace.

But Jennet is still alive. As I grab the telescope, her arm slips through the crook in mine, and she quickly steers me away from the cart.

"Come on," she whispers roughly in my ear, and I can feel her breath tickle my skin.

Don't need to ask you twice.

I let her drive me away from the smirking man, and as soon as we're out of earshot, she sighs in relief. "I was worried I wouldn't be able to hold up the illusion," she says with an amazed laugh.

"Illusion?"

She nods. "That wasn't real money I gave him." I blink at her in surprise, and she gives another snort. "Nothing too big, just a small spell to make it look like some paper was all the money he asked for."

Clever girl.

I try to glance back at the shopkeeper, but she puts a hand up to my jaw, forcing me to look down into those blue eyes. The gesture is close, intimate. Completely unexpected, and her eyes widen, as if surprised herself.

Then she recovers. "Don't look back at him," she says softly, averting her eyes. "Don't draw his suspicion."

Yeah, Rahym.

Right. Makes perfect sense. I don't want to see if he's noticed. That could only make it worse. "Did you learn that from the witches?" I ask, deftly changing the subject.

She slinks closer to me, twining her fingers with mine as we keep walking through the bazaar. Again, I swallow thickly, trying to think about anything other than her body up against mine. *Jennet is still here*, my mind tells me. *Jennet is still around.*

Like a ghost resurrected from my past.

"Yes," she says, and it takes me a moment to remember what question she's answering. "I've learned a few things from my tribe. Nothing too big...especially with the curse. But little parlor tricks to make things easier." She snickers. "Such as having an unlimited amount of cash." She nods to Fatma as we pass her buying bottles of vodka from a stall. The young witch smirks at us as she hands over some crisp bills.

"So all this money...?" I ask dumbly.

Jennet nods. "Being in a rebel group isn't exactly the most lucrative career."

So that explains how Nakir is going to be able to buy some horses or how any of us are going to be able to buy supplies. I doubt we'd be welcome in Derweze ever again after this.

You're assuming that you'll live after going through the Door.

True. Very true. This will probably be the last time I ever see this city. And I feel strangely *fine* with that.

It's not like anyone at the bazaar is going to miss you.

I snort out loud to myself, and Jennet peers up at me, curious. "And your ability to extend energy?" I ask, changing the topic. "Who taught you that?"

She regards me for a moment, her eyebrows raised in question. "That was all my own learning. And I haven't been able to teach it to anyone else. It just…happened one day."

"So there're no other witches who can do what you do?"

She shakes her head. "Fatma's specialty is sensing demonlings. Kerem can heal with his touch. And Sena can shield us from fire. But me?" She grins almost wickedly. "I'm the only one who can transfer energy."

No wonder Nakir thought he had a gold mine with her. If she was the first of her kind, then Jennet may be the only chance he has of making it. It's absurd, though, this whole thing. There's not much that a few hours of energy can do. Nakir would have to be able to fly to get to the Watchtower safely.

He's going to get her killed.

I clench my jaw and divert my attention away from her to the brother and sister duo as they pass by us. Jennet watches them, smiling softly as her eyes follow the two children. "You don't see kids much these days," she murmurs absently.

A shiver makes it way down my spine. "Too hard to raise

them," I say through too-dry lips. "You can't chase after them as much as you want. They need you when you can't help them. And as babies, they'll expend themselves crying in the middle of the night. You can't get out of bed to feed them. And when you think you've gotten a handle on it, they're taken from you, because you're too powerless to protect them."

Jennet doesn't say anything for a long moment as she watches them, a mixture of emotions crossing her face. "I'm so sorry."

I don't meet her eyes. "Beste would have been a little older than the girl. She was bright. Smart."

"She must have been a character."

The memory of my daughter pulls up the corner of my lips. "Just like her mother. And she had Maysa under her thumb."

"Must have not been fair to you."

"They'd always gang up against me. Two against one." I let out a short laugh, putting my hands on my hips with a slight shake of my head. "I'd give anything to have them back."

"Yes. I bet." She nods to the children still running around the bazaar, seemingly nowhere near slowing down. They shriek excitedly, completely unaware of the dangers surrounding them.

"They're why I'm doing this," she says softly, watching them.

"Children?"

"Yes." At my blank stare, she gives me a small smile. "Back in the old days, children were considered to be a sign of hope for the future. And if there aren't many children in the world, then there's no hope."

"Can you blame us?" I ask with a scoff.

She shrugs noncommittally. "I just want there to be a world where you don't have to worry about where you lay your head at night. Where you don't fall into a coma every day."

"And you think you'll be able to help?" I know I've asked the same question of her before, but her unfailing faith in the mission is...refreshing. I've given up, much like everyone else here, and this is my last hail Mary before I know I'll join Maysa and Beste in Paradise—why not throw it all away?

But Jennet truly believes.

"Hey." We both turn our heads to see one of the other Halos standing in the middle of the aisle, a man around my age that I haven't really gotten to talk to yet. Actually, I haven't really gotten to know any of the Halos. Introductions take energy, and while I could care less about my own amount of energy at any given time, I know that the others are more careful with how they spend their allotment. That kind of conservation doesn't leave much room for pleasantries.

And judging by the frown on this guy, I can tell he's not feeling pleasant at all. But Jennet smiles and gives him a slight wave.

"Hey, Murat," she hails him, and I can see as his gaze shifts from me to her. Protectively. Like he doesn't like me being this close to her. She doesn't address it, though, and instead says, "Did you find enough yurts?"

He dips his chin in affirmation. "Expensive, but I managed. Only three, though."

"That will have to do. Everything's expensive these days. We just paid ten thousand Manat for a telescope."

His dark eyes land on me again and narrow, taking me in. "Why the hell would you spend that much on a telescope?"

His voice is threatening. Accusing. And I can't figure out where the hell this hostility is coming from.

He sees you as competition for Jennet.

The thought brings a surprised smile to my face, and I beam over at him, which catches him off guard. Establish myself as the unstable, crazy person, and there won't be any trouble from him in the future.

I make a mental note to meet all the Halos now. The new number one on my list. As for anything else beyond that... well, life is so unexpected now, I'll cross that bridge when I get to it. *If* I get to it.

"They got it because I asked them to," Nakir says, materializing from the shadows like he does when he wants to *appear* mysterious. It does the trick, though, and Murat shies away from him. The fallen angel seems like he's in good spirits, though, and he gives us a wide grin. "So you got the telescope, Rahym?"

I pat the bag holding it. "Yeah. Did you find any horses?"

His smile widens. "Oh, I found something better than that. Far better."

CHAPTER 11

"Are those..." My words fumble over themselves as I look at the animals before me, the metallic sheen of their short hair gleaming in the sunlight. "Are those *Akhal-Teke horses?*"

Nakir crosses his arms, a proud smirk on his face. "Yep."

That bastard had managed to find one of the rarest horse breeds in the world. And not just one or two, either. *Ten* of them. Enough for every member of Halos to have their own ride. Ten of one of the rarest breeds of horses in the world. And I'm staring at them right now in shock. Both Nury and Kerem are loading them with supplies.

Ten Akhal-Teke horses. If I found out that the curse had been lifted overnight, I wouldn't be more surprised.

"I figured we'd need their endurance and their speed," Nakir says, walking up and giving a big grey stallion a pat on its nose. "They'll still fall prey to the Hibernation after four hours, but hopefully we'll go farther in that time than with other breeds."

"How the...?"

Jennet clears her throat, and I remember that she can conjure up counterfeit money. And that it's probably not a good idea to talk about it out in the open. I should have been able to remember that, but the horses in front of me are a distraction unlike any other.

Need to get your head screwed on right.

"Yeah, yeah," I mutter.

The sheer variation in the coloring of the animals reminds me just how beautiful my country's national horse. There are two chestnuts, a grey, a light palomino, a golden, and two dark bays, a cream-colored mare, and a spotted one.

One of the dark bay horses gives me a derisive sniff as I pass by it. "And you really think we'll be fine with them?"

"I'll take point, and then we'll keep the witches in the middle with the rest of the humans guarding them," Nakir tells me, keeping up with my pace as I stalk around the horses.

"Nice to know that we're expendable."

Well, what do you really have to offer?

I can offer grief, madness, and a weird sense of humor. That makes me lovable, right?

"I'm not going to lie to you, Rahym," Nakir says. "But I can tell you that the only way we'll be able to survive our trek into the Door is if none of the witches die. We need their powers to see us through."

I watch as Jennet helps Sena, the older witch, with a huge portion of food. "And Jennet?"

"She'll ride near me." At the harsh set of my jaw, he adds softly, "She's the most crucial component of our team. Without her, I don't know if we'll be able to make it."

It makes sense, even though I don't want to admit it. Nakir is the strongest fighter, by far. And with his abilities as an angel, Jennet couldn't be in safer hands. Except for the fact that I don't trust Nakir. Not after our last attempt to break the curse.

"If she dies," I mutter to him, "I'll kill you."

Nakir follows my gaze, a sad smile on his lips as he watches her interact with the rest of the members of Halos. She's taken a leadership position, delegating tasks and helping where it was needed. She'd always been like that, seeing what needed to be done. Maysa may have always put the needs of others before her, but Jennet instinctively knows what's right for the entire group.

"It doesn't matter," Nakir finally says, his voice grim. "If she dies, we're all dead."

CHAPTER 12

We find a Lodge on the outskirts of Derweze to spend our last night in the relative safety of the Door to Hell's shadow, far enough away from the bazaar so that when Jennet's magic on our money wears off, no one will chase after us. Which is a small comfort, because we're not so far away that if we *really* pissed someone off enough, they'd be after us in a heartbeat.

Such as stealing a telescope or ten Akhal-Teke horses.

Tomorrow, we'll go back to the same area where my own Lodge used to be, spend the night, and then head out at exactly midnight into the Door. And then take it in as few chunks as possible in order to get to Abaddon's Watchtower.

And from there? Jennet makes sure that Nakir is refreshed for killing Abaddon, and he does his thing. Done and dusted.

Except nothing is ever that easy.

To my utter surprise, I'm not the first to fall into Hibernation at the Lodge, despite my utter disregard for the amount of energy I spent today while shopping. Maybe my mental energy, expended by everything that happened in the past few days, isn't working in overdrive like it normally does.

So I take this time to unwind a bit.

In other words, I need a drink. I get up from my resting spot in the Great Room—smaller and less grand than the one in my Lodge, but it's a nice place to lay one's head.

The male witch, Kerem, has one eye open, watching me as I peel myself away from the chaise lounge that I had rested upon. His quiet mannerisms and big frame remind me of Yusuf, and I gulp self-consciously, trying to focus on something else.

Good luck. You're a mess.

"Shut up," I mumble, getting to my feet.

"You all right?" Kerem asks.

I wipe my hands on my trouser legs. "Yep. Just feeling antsy."

He gives me a crooked smile, and I'm not sure I like it, actually. It's almost...patronizing, and it sets my teeth on edge. "This will all be worth it in the end."

"Yeah, but you haven't seen what it costs," I tell him. "I have."

The smile doesn't falter. "We all have our reasons for being here," he simply says.

"This isn't a shitting contest," I tell him after fumbling for a comeback.

Why are you so bent on fighting the Halos?

Because I'm apparently a prickly asshole, that's why. I don't say anything else to Kerem—I'd rather conserve that bit of energy for another sip of vodka—and head to the bar, which is through a set of double doors and in another room, away from the main room. This Lodge is more rundown than mine was, which gives me an odd sense of pride.

We may have been living on the edge of sanity at my Lodge, but at least we presented ourselves nicely.

Nury and an older Halo are already at the bar when I park my own ass on a stool next to the young man. "Vodka," I say, slapping a real 5-Manat bill on the counter. Wouldn't do to piss off the bartender of the Lodge we're staying at. Especially with midnight leering nearby.

The man takes it without another word and quickly pours me a drink and puts it in front of me.

Quick and easy.

Nury holds up his drink in appraisal and tosses it back, wincing at the aftertaste. "Surprised you're still functioning," he says.

"I'm always up for cheap vodka. Like any normal person."

He frowns. "You're not a normal person."

It's an honest, genuine comment, and I bark a sharp laugh. "But I try. So hopefully no one notices."

"Oh, we noticed," the old man says with a huff as he takes a more measured drink. He doesn't waste the energy of grimacing at the taste. Maybe he drinks better vodka than I do.

Or maybe I can drink and be a hardass, too. I take a mouthful of my own glass of vodka and make a face despite my effort not to.

Nope. Definitely not a hardass.

The old man gives me a smug smirk at my reaction, the weathered lines of his face crinkling around his eyes, making him appear to be old. Far older than most people in my world grow to be. He must have been around from *before*.

My eyes widen at the realization. That maybe this man had been around when there was no curse. He has memories of a time when he wasn't counting his footsteps or worrying about how he'd make it to midnight.

"Where are my manners?" Nury says, breaking into my thoughts. "Rahym, I'm Nury. And this old man here is Emre."

We don't shake; we don't do things like that unless we need to, and while midnight isn't too far off, habit takes over. Instead, Emre just raises his eyebrows in answer.

"Yeah," I say. "You were in my group when the Lodge burned down."

Nury cringes. "Sorry about that."

Emre averts his eyes.

"Don't be. Not your fault." I take another swig of vodka and make another face. Again. "Fucking terrible grog, huh?"

Emre nods to the liquor bottles lining the bar. The bottles are dusty with some of their labels peeling off in the heat. "Vodka used to taste better than this. Way back when people had time to distill things properly. Nowadays, it's either you have the new shit stuff. Or," he taps a finger on the counter, "you have the old shit stuff with all the flavor evaporated out of it."

Bingo. He was older than the curse. I was right.

We were right. Shut up. I'd love to pick his brain, to hear what he has to say about the world before the curse.

"I've had worse," I say, gesturing to the drinks. "But I've also had better."

Emre chuckles and takes out another 5-Manat bill for the bartender. He doesn't even have to say what he wants before the bartender starts getting him another drink. Maybe he already knows what Emre wants. Or maybe it's all so terrible, it doesn't really matter.

"So why do you two have a death wish?" I ask. "You seem like you're too reasonable to follow Nakir into the Door."

There's a shocked pause from everyone, including the bartender, as he eavesdrops on our conversation before he resumes pouring the drink. Nury opens his mouth to answer but then coughs uncomfortably. Emre snickers.

"I'm an old man," he says, stating the obvious. "And I would do anything for my family." He twirls his finger to indicate the whole world outside. "I'd like to live to see it all go right. For their sakes."

"And…" Nury's voice trails off as his cheeks color.

"Nury's here to take care of a lady he's sweet on," Emre finishes for him.

I remember the knowing smile between Sena and Kerem. "You're talking about Fatma?"

Nury manages to turn an even more crimson shade, and I wonder if he'll go into Hibernation with his emotions in this high of a gear.

"Does she know?" I ask.

"Everyone but Fatma seems to know," Emre says, giving the younger Halo an encouraging clap on the shoulder. Nury presses his lips together.

I raise an eyebrow. "But you're on this trip because of her? And she doesn't know?"

"Well," he says, "I haven't gotten around to telling her yet."

It makes me realize just how much older I feel than Nury. And the age difference can't be that much—I'm in my early thirties, and Nury has to be in his early to mid-twenties. But there's an innocence and naivety about him that makes him seem much younger. It makes me feel far more world-weary. I've been married, had a child, and lost them both. He hasn't even worked up the nerve to tell the woman he loves how he feels about her.

How adorable.

I lean in toward Nury. "My advice? Life's too short. And being in Halos makes it much shorter than you want it to be."

The younger man meets my eyes. "You were in the original Halos, weren't you? 'Bout three years ago?"

Every cell in my body shudders to a halt, freezing the air in my lungs and causing my mind to go blank for a bit.

"Yes," I say finally through too-dry lips. "I was."

"How was that?" he asks, too eagerly. He puts both his elbows on the counter and leans over at me.

He thinks this is a hero's journey. That we'll be lauded if we came back. Have parades and statues and poems made in our names. He's romanticized it in his head, twisting it into something so far from the truth, it makes bile rise up in my throat, making it difficult to say anything.

"It was the biggest mistake of my life."

Both Emre and Nury watch me, going still at my honest answer. They don't prompt me to expand on it. Instead, their expressions turn from horror to sorrow.

"I'm not sure how much Nakir has told you," I rasp, swirling my drink. "If anything, I know the Door to Hell probably better than anyone else alive—and that's because they're all dead. I had a wife and a daughter. And I joined the Halos for a better future for them. Like you did, Emre," I add. The old man's cheeks flush. I scoff and shake my head. "Obviously it didn't work out. Otherwise we wouldn't be here."

"What happened?" Nury asks softly.

"Well," I say, not looking his way. "We started going into the Door, scouting out the various Door Stops. Going a little bit farther every time to see where we could go. We got cocky, went too far, and when the first Halo collapsed from the Hibernation, we turned back. We were too late. Demonlings attacked us a few miles out from my Lodge, where my wife and daughter were waiting for me. I tried making it back, for them. I collapsed about forty yards from them. And the demonlings brought the fire with them. It burned down the tree and front porch of the Lodge. The demonlings killed our horses. Maysa and Beste tried getting out of the Lodge, to save me. I can still remember them screaming before I passed out."

To punctuate my thoughts, my own memories play out the sounds of their voices, shrieking within the confines of my mind. I grit my teeth against it and give a slight shake of my head.

Don't focus on it. You can't change the past.

"I was burned all the way down my back," I say, touching my left side, where the skin is raised from third degree burns that I sustained. "But Maysa and Beste didn't make it, as well as all the other Halos." Like Sasha and Onsen. I gulp back the lump in my throat. "I swore then that I would continue Maysa's work. That her legacy would live on, not through our daughter, but through my work. And now the Lodge is gone, too."

They both watch me, and even the bartender has his full attention trained on me. But my story isn't unique. We all have our sob stories like mine in the world after the curse. We all know someone affected and killed by the curse and the demonlings.

It's Emre who speaks first. "I'm sorry."

I only nod.

Nury's eyes are so wide, I can see the white all around his irises.

"Yeah," I say. "It's not glamorous. People will die."

"But we have to try, don't we?" Nury finally asks. "For a better future."

So optimistic. So naïve. So all I give him is a noncommittal, "Maybe."

"So why are you doing this, then?" Emre asks, knowing that I'm not saying everything.

Smart man.

I give a shrug. "Seems to be the normal thing to do. At least by your standards."

Emre chuckles. "You're in the wrong crowd if you think we're normal. This guy may be on a quest to take care of his lady love." He nods to Nury. "But the rest of us? Eh." He shrugs dismissively. "You know Rabia? Big human woman with muscles?" I nod, remembering a Halo member fitting that description. "She's here because she lost her family at the Caspian Sea. They were on holiday at the beach, and..." His face trails off as he makes a face.

"Murat is here because his brother died with the original Halos," Emre says. I remember the man that had eyes for Jennet at the bazaar earlier. I'm surprised that I hadn't seen familial resemblance.

"Who was his brother?" I ask.

"Dunno," Emre says. "He doesn't talk about him too much. We understand why." I do, although I make a mental note to ask Nakir about it later. Maybe connecting with Murat would help us cross that chasm I felt at the bazaar.

Then again, if Murat already decided that he doesn't like you because you hang around Jennet...

Well, there are some things that being friendly can't fix.

"Sena, Fatma, and Kerem are here because of Jennet," Emre continues. "They know each other from when they were in their witch convent. And those witches stick together, apparently. As we know, Nury is here because of Fatma."

"And you? You said you were alive from before?"

Emre nods and picks up his new glass of vodka and takes

a sip before answering. "Yep. And I was in the army, too. So I saw firsthand what happened when chaos descended upon the world and our realms were split. Saw what happened when people fell into Hibernation. Saw the panic. The hysteria. And, well, I'm an old man now. Far older than I have a right to be in this apocalyptic world." He salutes me with his drink. "I'd like to see it return to the way it was."

"Well, I hope you live to see it that way."

"You don't think we will?" Nury asks, a hint of alarm edging into his voice.

He's so innocent, it almost makes me hurt from the inside out. This will probably be the first time he'll be in harm's way, the first time that he'll see that not everything works out all right in the end. The first time that he'll find out that heroes on a fool's journey are still fools.

Emre and I exchange a knowing glance. He's on the same page as me.

"We'll see," I say, giving the young man my best smile. "We're putting our best foot forward."

He doesn't seem to be comforted, so instead, I nudge his glass toward him.

"Drink up. For none of us know what tomorrow brings," I say.

"True statement," Emre adds, clinking his glass with mine.

After a moment's hesitation, Nury adds his drink to our toast. I'm able to get a full mouthful before the Hibernation overtakes me, my body's energy finally giving out from everything I did today.

I manage to set the glass down. "Think I'm at the end," I mutter before everything buckles, and I crumple to the floor of the sticky bar, unclean from years of neglect and other patrons passing out.

Maybe there won't be too many more times ahead where I'll pass out like this. And no one else will have to suffer because they have no control of their body from a curse.

Then again, I may just be headed toward a form of permanent Hibernation. And lying here, unable to move or do anything to protect myself, I'm terrified.

For the first time in three years, I realize that I don't want to die. I want to find joy in life again.

You want to succeed.

CHAPTER 13

M aysa digs her fingers into the dry, arid dirt before putting in a seed of…*something*. Her hands are smaller than I remember, and when she looks up, I realize why. She's ten years old again, her face free of the worry lines that started appearing just before she died. She's at the age right now where she's innocent enough to not realize the full extent of our predicament, but she's starting to realize that something's not right with the world.

"That's not going to grow there," I find myself saying, and it's a voice I almost don't recognize. It's my voice from when I was ten years old myself. I remember being a little shit. Mainly because I was trying to hide my conflicting feelings for Maysa. And Jennet. Two girls who made a prepubescent boy wonder if they were friends or more.

Maysa hums softly to herself, ignoring me. Her hair glints mahogany in the sunlight, pulled into a loose braid that has wisps floating in the breeze. She always smells of figs, and the scent assails my nose.

I breathe in deeply.

"Hey, Maysa," I say, reaching out to her shoulder. She looks up at me, from her crouch, her eyes golden. Even as a ten year old, she was beautiful in a delicate, fragile way. When she and Jennet were together in Derweze, they'd turn heads, even from those who were trying to conserve their energy.

"What, Rahym?" she asks.

I swallow back the lump in my throat. "Don't get your hopes up that this will grow."

"But it will." She nods down at the freshly dug earth. "It will grow. It has to."

I frown in confusion. "What did you plant?"

"A tree."

I let out a guffaw. "A tree? Out here?"

We both take stock of our surroundings. The desert sun is harsh and unforgiving as it bears down on us. We can see the glow of the Door to Hell, so perilously close, yet far enough to make us feel invincible. There's a wooden, two-story building next to us, the Lodge that Maysa's father is running. The building is old, but he's been renovating it.

It looks better at this point than any time I ever ran it. Maysa's father was just as proud of the Lodge as she was.

She saw a dream in it.

"We need some shade here," she says simply. "Even if they don't stay at the Lodge, someone may want to rest here."

"It'll take forever for it to grow," I mutter.

"That's fine."

"And you'll have to water it."

"That's fine, too."

"And you'll have to take care of it. And not let the Hibernation keep you from doing it."

"Yep."

I stop and chew the inside of my cheek, watching her.

Her conviction is refreshing. She believes this tree will have no problem growing. That everything will be fine.

"Rahym!"

We both look at the front of the Lodge, where I see my father standing next to Maysa's father. Jennet and her father are standing with them as well. Her blue eyes watch us intently, curious. She was stunning then, too. How did I never put together that she's a witch? There was something supernatural about her, even when we were ten.

How did a gangly, scruffy boy like me end up being friends with these two girls?

"Yeah, Pop?" I call out, getting to my feet.

"Time to go," my father says. "Mr. Ramazanov will bring Maysa next time they're in Derweze, so you'll see her next time."

I remember now. We dropped off deliveries from Derweze to the Lodge every other week. Maysa and her father would come to us in Derweze for the other weeks, so that they had a steady stream of supplies for the Lodge.

I look to Mr. Ramazanov, Maysa's father, and give him curt nod. "Sounds good. Thank you for having us, sir."

Jennet's blue-eyed gaze is on me, intense, before it shifts to Maysa. "Planting a fig tree?"

I never figured out how she knew it was a fig tree.

Maysa grins up at Jennet. "Yep."

"I hope it grows," Jennet says softly.

"Rahym, go help get the horses ready. We need to leave as soon as possible." Father sniffs the wind. "The Door is going to be full inferno tonight."

I nod as I hurry to the stables and help a servant saddle our horses to the carts. I'm cognizant that I need to conserve energy. Derweze is still fifteen miles out, and I don't want to fall into Hibernation before then.

Maysa's gone when I lead the horses out. In her place, Jennet stands over the place where she planted the seed. Her eyes glow with an otherworldliness as she turns to me. The light from them abruptly goes out as she smiles at me.

"I hope it grows," she says. "You know how much Maysa wants it to."

"Yeah," I say, transfixed by her, doubting what I had just seen. "What were you doing?"

Without another word, she pushes her way past me, and I'm by myself as the fig tree sprouts, its leaves growing at an impossibly fast rate. The trunk wraps around itself, twisting and growing as the fledgling plant turns into a tree that throws me in the shade.

I hear familiar laughter behind me—*Beste*—and I whirl my head at the sound, trying to locate it, to see my daughter one more time.

But the Hibernation overtakes me as the orange flickering from the Devil's Teeth grows in intensity. I collapse on my back to see the fire raining down from the sky. It catches the world around me in a blaze that blinds me. The heat scorches my skin, and I hear screaming.

Impossibly, even though the Hibernation has overtaken me, I know it's me.

You never could stop it. You tried everything you could.

And I watch as the tree—the tree that Maysa planted and that Jennet had spent some of her power helping to grow—catches fire.

And I wake up with a strangled cry. As I can move, it must be after midnight, but it's still dark outside, far enough from sunrise that no one else expends the energy to stir at my outburst. Sweat sticks my shift to my body. Someone took the energy to pluck me off the ground of the bar and put me in a bed at the Lodge in Derweze. Someone cared enough about me that I wouldn't spend the night in filth.

"Hey." I look over to see Jennet on a chaise across from me. "Are you all right?"

I swallow thickly as I give her a nod. "Yeah," I say. "Just nightmares."

She offers me a sad smile. "We all have those. It's a part of living in this world."

"I had a dream." I watch her. "Do you remember when Maysa planted that fig tree?"

Jennet nods. "Yes," she says softly.

"Did you...did you do something to help it grow?"

She meets my eyes and gives a slight nod. "Yes," she says, even softer. "Just a small spell, even before I knew I was a witch." She shifts away from me, as if self-conscious that her secret had been found out. "But...I didn't want her hopes being dashed. We had enough of that growing up."

I close my eyes. "Thank you for that," I whisper.

There's a pause before Jennet replies. "Anything for Maysa."

CHAPTER 14

"Rahym? Rahym, are you all right?"

It's two days later, and I blink a couple times and turn my head toward the person speaking to me. The younger witch, Fatma, is watching me intently from the back of a cream-colored horse. The witch's big brown eyes watch me curiously, concern etched into her beautiful features. Like Nury, there's an innocence about her, like she truly believes that we'll get through this on the other side.

"I'm fine," I say through dry lips.

No, you're not.

No, I'm not fine.

We're a hill away from where my Lodge is—*was*—and all I can think about is the fact that I'm so close to my home. Where I spent the happiest years of my life with Maysa and Beste. And now it's burned to the ground.

I'm not sure I can do this.

You have to. Everyone is counting on you.

We suddenly take our horses perpendicular to the worn

path that runs by my Lodge. Toward the Door to Hell. Away from my memories.

And toward your death.

The change in temperature is almost immediate. With every step toward the Door to Hell, the heat inches up degree by degree. I'd almost forgotten how oppressive the heat can be, even before you enter the Door.

It'll be the last thing you feel.

I want to shout at the voice in my head to shut up and leave me in peace. Shut up, shut up, *shut up!*

"—hym? Rahym?" It's Nury this time as he brings up his horse next to the young witch and me.

"I'm fine," I repeat again, steering my big brown bay away from them, wanting to get away from their concern and their eyes. I kick my horse to a canter to catch up with Nakir at the front of our group. The horse is named Alion, which must be an ironic name, as it means "friendly," and this guy is definitely not friendly. He huffs in irritation at me and pulls at the reins, fighting me the entire way.

He's a headstrong asshole. Which I think is part of the reason I was paired up with him. Everyone else seems to be getting along with their horses except for me and friendly Alion.

"C'mon," I mutter to him, bringing up alongside Nakir.

The angel peers over at me. "Rahym?" He looks behind us, as if trying to figure out what's happening. "What's wrong?"

"I want a new horse. This one is broken."

Nakir bursts out laughing. "That's not how it works."

"Why not?" I click my tongue in anger as Alion tries to veer in a different direction. "He's going to wear himself out fighting me the entire way, and he's going to drain my energy doing it. Hence—he's broken."

"It's just because he can sense that you're irritated," the angel chides. Both Alion and I snort at the same time in answer, and Nakir grins. "You're two of a kind."

I focus on my anger toward the beast, because it helps me take my mind off the Lodge that's so close by. Maybe Alion being as stubborn as a mule will be a good thing. And maybe that's why Nakir paired us up.

Maybe he gave you a horse that acts like a child because you act like a child.

"Heaven knows you need to learn patience," Nakir adds amusedly.

"Heaven knows you need to learn humility," I shoot back as Alion decides to trot at a diagonal trajectory, just because he's being an asshole. Nakir's gaze turns soft as he watches us.

"Yes," he murmurs, his expression wistful. "Yes, I do. Had I learned that, we would have been successful years ago."

And suddenly we're both silent as we reflect on the past. On the Halos that we lost three years ago.

Rahym Tezel. Killer of conversations.

"I think about them all the time," Nakir says softly. "About what I could have done differently to save them. To save Maysa and Beste. I was...cocky." He rakes a hand through his short, black hair, ruffling it in the front. "I just...I wish..."

Wishing doesn't change the past.

I clear my throat uncomfortably. "What's Heaven like?"

We clomp along in silence as he mulls over his words before answering. Finally, he sighs and glances back at me. "To be honest, what I remember of Heaven is probably a lot different than what it is now. I fell a long time ago."

"Why?" I blurt the question out before I can stop it.

Rahym Tezel. Initiator of awkward conversations.

Nakir doesn't mind me prying, though. I guess he owes

me that much. "I fell in love with a human woman."

"Oh," I say. I should have guessed. Even though I'd considered myself a good friend of his back with the original Halos, I'd never heard this story from him. How an angel of God fell to Earth and ended up cursed with the rest of our unlucky lot.

"Her name was Irem—*Heaven.*" He grimaces at the memory as he rubs at his back, where I know the stumps of his wings still bleed beneath bandages that he wears every day. Still hurt him. "She was my heaven. And I'd gladly fall again for her. But she was painfully mortal. And we both know how mortality can take those we love from us."

He sighs and sits back in his saddle, his horse not even flicking an ear in irritation. Meanwhile, Alion gives me the evil eye.

"Did you…?" I lick my lips. "Did you start a family with her?"

Nakir shakes his head. "No. Angels can't have families. Not like that. I didn't know that I was immortal back then. Thought I'd join her after my time was up here. Apparently, my time must not be up yet." He huffs angrily, glancing up at the sky. "I guess I've been roaming here just for this opportunity. To save us from this curse."

I nod to the sword strapped to Nakir's back. "Do you really think that the Sword of Jan is enough to break the curse?"

"I've been carrying this thing for thousands of years. It's the only thing that can kill a demon. It *can* stop Abaddon," he says with such conviction, I flinch. "It *will* stop the curse. I know how precious life is, Rahym. I know you think I didn't mourn the Halos we lost. I know you think I'm leading this group to their deaths as well." He nods at the riders behind us.

I don't reply, because he knows me so well.

"But trust me when I say," Nakir says, giving me a meaningful glance, "that after seeing so much death and destruction in my life, I know there is still a world worth saving here. And I'm willing to risk my life to see it returned that way. What's been broken can be fixed. Even hearts."

I follow his gaze towards Jennet as she rides point with her group of witches. She talks with them, her smile exuberant, just how I remember it from our childhood. I know what he's getting at, but I don't know if I can bring myself to admit it.

That maybe there is life after a broken heart.

"Why did you join Halos this time around?" Nakir asks me point blank.

My lips are dry as I try to speak. But I can't take my eyes off Jennet. "I..."

He doesn't wait for me to string together a coherent sentence. "You haven't given up on living yet. Even though you've convinced yourself you have." His jaw tightens. "Neither have I. Even after thousands of years."

I look back at him, feeling that sensation in my chest again. Hope?

Shit, you'd better hope not.

We crest another hill, where the heat gets even more intense, and even breathing gets harder to do. How the hell did I use to work as a miner here? It feels almost alien to me, like this is a place completely separate from Earth.

Before us, the Door to Hell opens up in a wide crater. It's a deserted wasteland that stretches as far as we can see. Fires spew uncontrollably, spitting out of cracks in the soil. There are some shaded areas—the Door Stops, where travelers can find respite for a time—but it's barren, desolate, and lifeless. I don't even see any demonlings roaming, but that doesn't mean they're not there. I learned a long time ago that demonlings can be hiding even in the sand.

And at the very edge of the horizon, beyond the haze, is the dark tower that stretches up from the far edge of the crater, like a scar on the plains.

Abaddon's Watchtower. The source of the curse.

No one's ever been there and lived to tell the tale.

"I remember the days when there wasn't a tower there," a voice says, joining us at the lip of the crater. Emre pulls his mare up next to mine, and he gestures toward the hulking structure.

"I remember those days, too," Nakir says grimly.

I have trouble trying to conceive of a time where I didn't have Abaddon's Watchtower. I've lived in its shadow all my life, had nightmares about it when I was child. And as a full-grown adult. It's haunted every single movement I've made my entire life.

"How do we even know that's what caused the curse?" Nury asks as he steps by us. The others are catching up to us now, the whole mood somber as we see the journey before us.

"Because," the female named Rabia says, her jaw clenched, "it showed up with the curse."

Emre nods. "It just appeared out of nowhere when we all fell victim to it. And the Door to Hell became…well, *this*…" He spreads his hands out to indicate the wasteland before us.

Here, with all of the Halos, I feel like this is the calm before the storm that we're about to get swept up in. I lean into Nakir, so that he's the only one who can hear my question.

"Do you really think we can do it? Do you think we can break the curse?"

Nakir meets my eyes and gives me a slow nod. "We wouldn't be here if I didn't."

CHAPTER 15

I can't imagine how much hotter Hell must be, because being at its Door is like trying to live in a brick oven. The heat is ever-present, ever-oppressive, and ever-fucking-irritating. It feels like I'm breathing through a straw and like my skin is blistering from the heat. Sweat drenches me, making me feel like I've just been dunked in a vat of hot water. My ears burn with the dry wind, a low roar that overtakes every other sound.

There's no way to escape it. Even Alion has stopped fighting me and is trying to just keep one hoof in front of the other. We all are.

And then there are the fires that pop up all over the place. I try imparting some helpful tips to the Halos, but it feels like I'm just talking to myself. Literally.

"You have to keep your eyes on the ground. Fires will break through where the earth is thinnest. You'll feel your horse slipping a bit before it erupts, so you have a few seconds to get out of the way."

Thanks. One good bit of advice.

"Demonlings hide in holes in the ground, unless they're on the move. And if they are, you'll see the sand they kick up."

Unless they've gotten smarter at hiding those trails.

The Halos have fallen silent trying to conserve their energies. If it weren't for the curse, I think we'd still be silent. It takes too much to do anything other than focus on not passing out from heat exhaustion.

But I fight it, because I want to. I'm not a smart man. Stubborn, maybe, but not smart.

Hibernation isn't too far away, either. I can sense it always there, taunting me. If we take one step out of line, then we're dead.

Hell, if you take one hair out of line, you're dead. And no one will mourn you.

I wonder how much mental energy that other voice of mine takes up. Imagine how much more I could have done in my life if I didn't have to silence that damn thing every three seconds.

You needed the company.

I snort.

"Sena!" I hear Jennet cry. "Sena!"

There's an answering thump as we all turn to see the elderly witch fall off her horse, unconscious from the Hibernation. Luckily, Kerem is near enough to catch her before she falls all the way to the ground. He gives a rough grunt as he takes on her weight, and I can tell that he's fighting off the Hibernation as well.

We've reached our limits too quickly. Too fast. At this rate, it will take us days to get to the Watchtower.

"Rahym," Nakir says sharply, looking at me. He's been keeping Alion and me toward the front of the group. I'm supposed to be leading them, after all. Because I'm some sort of expert on the Door. "We need to find a Door Stop. For the night."

Right. For the night. I've spent a grand total of two nights in the Door to Hell before I had to find my way back to civilization. I pull the map out of my satchel, where I'd earlier added to it with all of Door Stops that I can remember. Even being here right now, I can tell that the map is either horribly out of date, or the mapmaker didn't know the area well enough to make a great map.

Then again, no one knows the Door at all. They've all died.

I gulp back the rock that's somehow wedged its way in my throat. "There's one about a half-mile..." I fumble for a moment and pull out the compass. Sweat drips on both the compass and the map, smearing the ink to near obscurity.

Hopefully we won't need to stay at that *Door Stop.*

"A half-mile that way," I say, pointing in a northwest direction. "According to the map, at least."

Nakir narrows his eyes.

"I've stayed there myself," I tell him to add credence, although that's a lie borne out of desperation to get us moving. I'd never been to that particular Door Stop before, and I don't know why I bent the truth, but there it is.

I think he knows it's a lie, too. But he gives a gruff nod and points the way.

That's enough for everyone to spur their horses. I nicker to Alion to follow, and he doesn't protest. Time and energy is leeching from everyone as we hurry, our predicament bearing down on us like the heat.

For a horrified moment, I don't see anything that resembles a Door Stop, and I wonder if I've misled the entire group toward something that doesn't even exist. If so, then I caused their deaths this time. I'd be just as responsible as Nakir.

I let out a relieved breath as the shaded area comes into view, obscured by a dune that blended in with the rest of our stark surroundings. It's a small one, but it's large enough for us to spend the night and keep the horses safe.

"We spending the night *there*?" Murat shouts, giving me an angry glare.

If he doesn't like it, he can spend it where he wants.

I agree and hide my smirk as I spur Alion on faster and faster. Are we expending too much energy in this last burst? Will we get there without collapsing?

"Demonling!" Fatma cries out, her voice anguished. "There's a demonling nearby."

Good to know that her gift is still working. And good to know that we'll make it to the Door Stop to avoid the demonlings.

There.

At the Door Stop, I see an ugly fucker rear his head at the lip of the sheltered area. *Of course.* A demonling would also use the Door Stops as a place to rest. And it's using the same one we are trying to hole up in as our energy fades.

This isn't going to go very well.

I see Murat by me recoil in horror at the sight of the demonling, rearing his horse back as it whinnies. The other Halos do the same, frightened at the sight of the monster in front of us. As well they should be.

But we don't have time for that shit.

I pull out my yataghan from its scabbard, hearing the metallic *snick* as I raise it high. Alion's a good enough sport to not stumble or misstep as he keeps running toward the Door Stop. Maybe this horse and I will get along after all.

We just have to see if we can survive this.

Sweat makes my shirt cling to me, and I grit my teeth as we get closer, closer. The demonling screeches at seeing me. I don't slow down. Alion doesn't slow down. I leap from his back, sweeping down my yataghan in an arc. The blade catches the demonling by surprise—I guess he was expecting me to stop or dismount or something, but I don't have the energy nor the time to do that—and his face splits in two. Hot, black blood spurts from his wound and splatters on my face. The demonling isn't screeching now—he's *screaming*.

Good job.

"Thank you," I mutter before I drive the blade through the thing's chest all the way to the hilt. The demonling looks at me, his eyes wide open in shock. "Sorry about that," I tell him, out of remorse, I think.

Not that he was planning on sharing the Door Stop with us. I've dealt with so many demonlings in my time as a miner, it's better to catch them unawares like this rather than try sparing them. He'd just come back later when we were in the throes of Hibernation. With friends.

He snarls one last time before he dies.

I pull out the blade, and the demonling crumples to the ground. The other Halos trot up to the Door Stop, some of their mouths open in shock or awe.

I wipe some blood off my face and give them a toothy grin, my gaze finding Jennet's in the crowd. "Another thing," I tell them, straightening up, "is that you can't hesitate. Demonlings won't play nice with you."

My yataghan leaves my fingers as my grip slackens, the Hibernation deciding now is a good time to take over. I give one last smile to Jennet before I collapse.

CHAPTER 16

I'm greeted by the crackling of a fire when I wake up—too close for comfort, especially in the Door to Hell. My instincts kick in at how close danger is to me while I was in Hibernation.

"Run!" I shout, my eyes going wild. "Run, you idiots—!"

A strong hand presses against my chest and pushes me back down to the floor. "Relax, Rahym. This is just our campfire." *Jennet*. She gently smiles down as the pressure of her hand against my chest increases. I'm fighting her. I need to stop.

I take a few moments to get my breathing under control, swallowing back the lump in my dry throat. "Campfire?" I ask. "Why do we have a campfire?"

"We have to eat, don't we?" Fatma asks, and I twist my head to look at her. She sits crouched in front of the fire, stoking the flames with a sword. It's only now that I see the hunks of meat roasting on a jerry-rigged spit.

"We figured with all the fires nearby, it would help us

blend in," Jennet says with a shrug. "Demonlings don't seem to like fire anyway."

"The smell will call them," I remind her. "They like cooked meat just as much as we do."

"Speak for yourself," the male witch named Kerem says with a snicker. He bites into an apple. Vegetarian, then. You don't see too many of those when desperation leads you to eat whatever's at hand. There are a lot of people who don't want to eat meat, but with energy in such short supply, if you set a plate of chicken in front of them, they'll gladly eat it.

"We're keeping an eye on everything," Emre says, nodding out over the hills. "Fatma's keeping her senses out looking for other demonlings, and Rabia and Nury are on watch."

I nod, knowing that we'll have to tie ourselves to our saddles tomorrow to keep ourselves aloft.

"Besides," Nakir says, walking over to Jennet and me. "I'm thinking that we should try making our way to the next Door Stop before the sun rises to avoid the heat and the exhaustion that comes from it."

"No," I say, struggling to sit up. Nakir frowns at my short answer. "Because we wouldn't be the only ones thinking that. The demonlings are out in full force at night, because it's so damn hot during the day. And we'll expend all our energies before the sun rises, and you don't want to have that long between when you pass out and when you're rejuvenated."

"I'm just thinking that it would make the most logical sense that way," Nakir says, his jaw twitching.

I level him with my gaze. "And you came to me because I'm a so-called expert at the Door to Hell. So trust me when I say—traveling the daytime, as much as it sucks, is a much better option than trying to compete with these assholes out there. You think one is bad. Wait until you come up against a whole herd of them."

Or whatever it is you call a group of demonlings.

Maybe a flock. Or a gaggle. That makes them sound ridiculous, so I'm going with that. Ridiculous gaggle of demonic assholes.

Nakir doesn't say anything, but I can see that he's contemplating my words. I know I'm right. Hell, he knows I'm right. Traveling at night is the first mistake anyone makes with the Door to Hell. It lulls you in, because you can't handle the heat.

But that's the worst time to try.

"What time is it, anyway?" I mutter, looking around.

"Just after midnight," Jennet answers quickly. "You've been out for around four hours."

Just after midnight, so we'd have another full twenty-four hours before we're up again. I look around at everyone who is still up and doing things. It only seems like Rabia and Sena are still asleep. Everyone else is watching over the edge in case a demonling or some fire spreads our way. The horses are tied up, not moving too much, which is a good sign. Hopefully they'll conserve their strength.

As I've mentioned to Nakir, the Door Stops don't offer much in the way of protection. Someone thought they were clever when they came up with the name, but they're really just the undersides of enormous rocks in the desert, offering little coves and caves within them. Some are merely just protected on three sides. Others—like the one we're currently staying in—are actually like little caves, with the rock overhanging and offering up much more protection. This one is one of the better ones I've seen, so while everyone else looks like they're anxious and alert, I feel pretty calm and at ease.

But they are going to wear themselves out if they keep this up.

"We should take turns," I say. "Only one person awake while the others rest. Otherwise, we're not going to make it."

Jennet's eyebrows push together, but Nakir nods. "You're a crazy son of a bitch," he mutters as he moves away from us, telling the others to try to sleep. I almost grin at that.

There's some vodka somewhere. I want to tell him to use it to get people to sleep. They may be hungover in the morning, but sometimes, that's the only way you can sleep in the Door to Hell.

Jennet stops me, though, not with an action or anything, but with a silent, reproachful look.

"What?" I ask.

"You attacked that demonling without any regard for yourself," she says softly. "When you were so close to Hibernation."

She's right. Another second or a moment's hesitation from me and I would have passed out before killing the demonling.

"You can't hesitate in the Door to Hell," I tell her.

"Yes, but…" Her voice trails off. "You had nearly…nearly…"

I shrug. "I have little regard for myself," I say, trying to be as nonchalant as possible.

She watches me for another moment. "I know you think you have something like a death wish, but don't you dare waste your life like that."

"Even though you're throwing away yours?" I counter. Her eyes widen in shock, and I know I've hit her below the belt. Figuratively speaking, since she's not a man.

"We're all just trying to save the world," she says softly.

"And hesitation will get you killed," I say, bristling. "As I told Nakir, you all came to me for help. My advice? Don't hesitate, and run. And live your life, Jennet."

I had meant for her to get angry at me for my hostile tone, for putting her down like that. Anything to push her away, because I know what's happening. I don't want her to get hurt. But instead, she watches me for a moment longer before patting my shoulder, surprising me that she's not getting angry.

"Just don't do that again," she whispers. "Don't think your life doesn't have meaning."

Her hand lingers on me, and I feel that comforting sensation of heat in my shoulder again. I feel a flicker of my energy grow. Her hand glows for a brief moment before she pulls back. She opens her mouth to say something but instead closes it and moves away from me.

Leaving me with conflicted feelings and a warm spot on my shoulder. I bite my lip as I watch her, a different kind of warming sensation blossoming in my chest.

Shit.

No, I'm not allowed to feel this way. Not after Maysa and Beste's deaths. Not when we're both so close to our own deaths.

Not when you're broken into so many pieces you won't ever be good enough for her.

"Rahym." I turn my head to see Nakir back, looking haggard and tired.

"What?"

"Come with me."

"But the energy. The—"

"I want to show you something. Bring the telescope with you."

I dig it out of my saddle bags, not wanting to expend the energy arguing with him—especially since Jennet spent some of hers on me—and I follow him. He walks me toward the edge of the Door Stop, where the divot we're in overlooks the rest of the Door to Hell. From here, we can see out over the dark desert, spotting the different wildfires burning out of control. The full moon illuminates the landscape, and between that and the wildfires, I feel like we can see a lot of the landscape. I see the dark clouds moving across the desert too, so close to the ground that, if you don't know what they are, you'd think they are dust devils or small tornadoes. No, these are gaggles of demonlings moving along the desert, attacking anything they come across.

There are lots of those dust clouds, some much bigger than others. And I'm so glad that we're at a Door Stop right now. Beyond the known map in my mind of the Door, I hope there are enough to get us to the Watchtower.

"Hand it to me," Nakir says, and without waiting for me to react or respond, he takes the telescope from me anyway. He points it northwest of us, in the direction that we're going and goes completely still.

"Was it worth ten thousand Manat?" I mutter sarcastically.

"Yes," Nakir says with complete conviction. "Even if we paid for it with real money."

"Why?"

"For this."

He hands it to me, and as I put my eye up to the eyepiece, he directs my gaze. With everything magnified through the telescope, I'm able to see places that I've never had a good look at—during the day or night. There's the Lion's Rock, which looks like a mythical lion's head overlooking the plains. Some thought it was a Door Stop until they were entrapped in some quicksand there. There's the Table Plateau, a place where it looks like a flattened tabletop. And so many others.

"Do you see the Watchtower?" Nakir asks.

I swerve toward it, a big black obelisk that rises over the desert, taller than any building in Derweze or Merve. Abaddon's Watchtower could be seen from miles away, and most of my work as a miner was in its shadow. I've just never had the chance to see it like this. From here, I can see that the tower itself is shiny, like it's made entirely out of obsidian. Various balconies and windows dot the sides at erratic intervals, where firelight emanates from within. I wonder how big the demon is that lives there. How many others live there.

And why they hold such sway over us.

Seeing it like this gives me a sense of vertigo, that we have to go through *that*.

"Yeah I see it. Why?"

"That's the real reason I wanted the telescope," Nakir says with a sigh. I wanted to see if I could see Abaddon."

I look away from the view to face him directly, and there's a strong set to his jaw as he looks at the tower, the fires reflected in his dark eyes. "Why the hell would you want to see him?"

At first, he doesn't answer me. *What a time to suddenly decide he wants to conserve energy.* Finally, he does speak, and it's the last thing I expect to hear from him. "I want to see if he's still the Abaddon I knew."

"Wait, you *know* Abaddon? The monster that has haunted us for over fifty years now?" No wonder he was able to talk about the Demon Lord who is the source of our curse. The angel *knows* him personally.

Nakir nods. "*Knew* him, yes. He was like a brother to me. Once upon a time."

I open my mouth to say something, but shock tightens my throat, and I can't speak. Because...the implications of Nakir knowing Abaddon are…huge. All that comes out is a pathetic, "How… Why? *How?*"

Nakir eyes me warily. "We were in Heaven together. He was there from the beginning. We'd do anything for each other. Spent millennia helping each other."

"What happened?"

He smirks. "Remember that I said I fell in love with a human woman?"

"Yeah?"

"When I fell, he rebelled against God. In my defense." He crosses his arms, his expression fierce as he looks back at the tower. "He did it in my honor. And while I fell to earth, he fell even farther than me. He became a demon because of me, Rahym. And I feel responsible for that. It's all because of me. And I wanted to see if there's any shred of the Abaddon I once knew." He indicates the telescope with his head. "I was hoping to get another glance at him."

"And this is the first time you're telling me of this?" I ask incredulously.

"It's not something that needs to be broadcasted," Nakir answers softly.

"Well, this changes everything."

"It changes nothing," he snarls at me. "We still have a curse to break. We still have to make it to the Watchtower. And if Abaddon doesn't relent, I'll have to kill him."

"And you're so sure that you'll be able to kill him?" I throw up my hands in frustration. "You just told me he was like a brother to you."

"I will do what I must," Nakir says, unmoving from his stance.

"I find that hard to believe," I scoff.

Me too.

"Right," I mutter with a nod, shaking the porridge from

my head. Nakir frowns at me. "After all, you spent ten thousand Manat on a telescope."

"It wasn't real money."

"You told me that it would have been worth it even if it were real money." I narrow my eyes. "Do you still have feelings for Abaddon? Misplaced camaraderie?"

"It will tell us of Abaddon's movements," he says, blinking. As if trying to convince himself of it. It's the first time I've truly seen him unravel even the slightest. He's really torn up over Abaddon's current state. "If we need to be on alert otherwise. If we need to keep an eye out for him."

I look through the telescope again, back at the Watchtower. "And you think that we should be more concerned about Abaddon than the demonlings?"

"Abaddon will be much harder to kill than demonlings," Nakir mutters softly.

I scan over the desert, pausing momentarily as I see other shapes moving along the dunes, heading our way. "Possibly," I say. "But I think I just found another use for your telescope."

Maybe Nakir wants it for his own reasons, borne out of a need to see the brother-figure he'd lost a long time ago. But now I see an entirely different reason for it. And this definitely makes it worth ten thousand Manat.

"Where's the demonling corpse?" I ask, turning back to the campsite. "The one I just killed?"

"It's over there," Nakir says, confusedly. He points to the exact opposite side of the Door Stop. "We threw it out because it stinks."

The stink is exactly why I need it. I bound through the campsite, over sleeping bodies. I spot a spear among our weapons stash and grab it as I grab my yataghan, a madman on my quest. I find the demonling just outside the Door Stop, hidden in the shadows. I forgot how badly they smell, how horrible of an assault they are on your nose.

I pull back the demonling's head and give it two whacks with the yataghan to sever it from the rest of the body. Apparently, I'm much better at hacking apart demonling corpses than burned trees, which is a sad thought in and of itself, but I guess it comes in handy right now.

The demonling's thick, coagulated blood drips in large globs as I pull the head away from the body with a squelching sound. I take the end of the spear and stick it through the remains of the neck. It's sickening work, but I remind myself that it's necessary.

I run back to the other edge of camp.

"Hey!" Fatma yells after me, a look of disgust on her face at my makeshift warning sign.

"Your little gift about sensing demonlings nearby is apparently very limited," I snap at her.

Why are you holding this against her? She's supposed to be asleep.

Maybe that's why. Or maybe because I'm freaked about how close we are to catastrophe. We're on a thin line, toeing disaster at every opportunity.

She only looks at me, aghast, as I run past Nakir, grabbing the telescope, and stop at the outer edge of the Door Stop. I check the telescope one last time before driving the butt of the spear into the sand, expending way too much energy on trying to make it stand upright. But I manage after some difficulty, the demonling's face pointing outwards, its mouth permanently open and the stink almost unbearable.

I check the telescope again and see the gaggle of demonlings halt, sniffing the air slightly. They smell their fallen comrade, even if they don't know him personally. Even though they're miles away, I see the leader of the horde pause, baring his teeth our way. This one is ugly too, and through the telescope, I can see him clearly.

It's a grisly thing I had to do, but it does the job, because the demonling signals the group to stop advancing our way and change direction. He gives one last glance at me, narrowing his eyes before turning and stalking away from the group.

He could have easily used fire against us and initiated a battle, but he didn't. Maybe I scared him off. Or maybe he'll come back stronger. Angrier.

Either way, there won't be a fight between us tonight.

I let out a breath of relief and make my way back toward the Door Stop. I toss the telescope to Nakir, who catches it deftly.

"We've already found its worth," I tell him. "We should keep it handy in case the demonlings decide to attack later."

Alion huffs at me as I walk by him and find a patch a land that I can spend the rest of the night sleeping on. I don't bother with a tent—I think my little stunt of running back and forth to ward off other demonlings is enough energy spent for the rest of the night. I need to conserve as much as possible.

And as I try to fall asleep, I see that Emre is watching me, even though he's meant to be asleep as well.

He gives me a slight nod, and I can't help the smile that breaks on my face.

One day down. And tomorrow's another long day. Another day of impossibilities.

CHAPTER 17

J ennet hoists her pack over her shoulder and stops at the sight of the demonling's head. A flit of different emotions passes over her face as she looks at it, from pity to disgust. At me, I think for doing such a barbaric thing, and I feel the shame spread across my cheeks as she glances at me.

I feel like she sees right through me, all the way to my insecure heart.

She finally takes a breath, sighs, and then pushes past me.

"Don't lose yourself on this journey, Rahym," she murmurs, her voice so soft, I wonder if I imagined it. But then she looks directly at me and says, stronger, "Don't become a demon yourself."

I watch after her as she pulls herself up into her horse's saddle and turns away from me. Even though she grew up near this area, there are still so many things she doesn't understand. I clench my fist, realize that I'm expending too much energy—mental and physical—and release it with a deep sigh. I comb a hand through my hair, which is already sweaty from the heat, before bending over to grab my own bag and mount Alion.

"You can tell those who have never seen battle," Emre tells me, a small smirk on his face. "She doesn't know that you sometimes have to do things that make your skin crawl for the greater good."

"No, she's right," I tell him as I clench my jaw and give a curt nod. "She's right."

I only have one item on my list today: *1. Survive.* Which, given our current predicament, seems nearly impossible.

You just have to brave the heat, avoid demonlings, find a Door Step before you collapse, not veer off in the wrong direction, and keep everyone else alive too.

Hence, it's all under the one umbrella of "survive."

No wonder it seems so hard.

The demonling's head is even more gruesome in the daylight, its mouth hanging open in a frozen scream. Its blood has coagulated down the pole of the spear, darkening the sand around it. I guess that's one spear we won't take with us. We could take it with us to ward off other demonlings from getting any ideas, but...the smell is so bad, my eyes water as I pass it. Even Alion huffs and skitters away from it.

Just like you after you haven't bathed in a month.

"Hey, that was just one time," I say, rolling my eyes. I see that Emre hasn't left my side, as he watches me silently, his lips pressed together in a thin line as he mulls over these events.

It's a fact of life I've had to live with since before Maysa and Beste were killed. Being so close to the Door to Hell, I have to know how to deal with these monsters every day and what to do if they ever attack.

It's worth it to protect Jennet, I've decided. Worth it, and

I'd do it again. Even if she hated me for stooping to the level of the monsters around us.

I catch another whiff of the demonling's head and crinkle my nose. Yep, definitely not taking that thing with us.

We trek through the desert in the silence. Even my mind is quiet as our horses clomp along, which is a nice for a change. I feel like I'm hanging on by threads as my anxiety and fear are heightened the entire time I'm here. I'd spent the night in a relatively fitful state of rest—you never ever truly relax while you're in the Door to Hell, so the longer you're here, the more you drain yourself. The time is ticking, making us weaker as time goes on.

We have to keep going. The Watchtower seems both so close and so far from us, and no matter how far we travel, it seems like we're the same distance away from it. Or even farther away, but that may just be my own desperation coming into play.

Jennet keeps her mare ahead of Alion, riding beside Nakir and the other witches. She glances back every so often at me, her expression guarded except for the slight pinch of her eyebrows as our eyes meet. Every time it happens, a few heartbeats pass before she shifts back in her saddle and talks with everyone by her.

Excluding me. It shouldn't hurt, because I shouldn't care what she thinks about me. But it does, and that feeling in my chest twists and aches just a bit.

Just as well.

I roll my eyes. "Was wondering when you'd show up."

Was wondering when you'd stop feeling sorry for yourself.

And despite everything, I grin. I see that Jennet's looking back at me again, obviously hearing my conversation to my inner workings. She quirks an eyebrow, her own lips pulling up in amusement, but she turns back to the front as Sena tells her something. Jennet answers, and the other witches laugh. Watching her interact with them is…something else. I can tell that the others have a lot of respect for her. I'm not sure what life was like for her when she moved to live with the other witches, but they care for her. And she cares for them, too.

I hope they aren't broken apart after this journey.

You're putting too much pressure on yourself.

Well, I've been here before. I know what happens when people get too hopeful about breaking this curse. I know what it feels like to have those you care about die before your very eyes. And the nature of our curse makes it very hard to do anything about it when we're spent.

I sigh and comb a hand through my hair, mussing it up so it stands straight up. We're all sweaty and too hot and dirty from yesterday. Yet another thing that's going to wear on us throughout our trip into the Door. I forgot how shitty this feeling is, and every moment is a new reminder of it.

Nury brings his horse up close to mine, so close that I turn my head and blink at him curiously. You don't get this close to someone unless you want something from them.

"Yeah?" I ask.

Nury blinks at my shortness, then nods to the group ahead of us. "Is it safe for them to be up front? I thought they were the most important part of all the Halos."

"They're witches," the human female named Rabia says as she kicks her heels into her horse to make it trot faster. "They don't really need our protection." She's a big woman and speaks even less than Kerem, so I haven't had much interaction with her, but she seems steady enough on her horse. I'm sure she knows how to swing the swords strapped to her back—and I wouldn't want to ask to make double sure, because she has this fuck-off attitude that tells me to keep quiet.

But Nury doesn't know to not push her. "Still though—we can't take any chances, right?"

Rabia snorts. "I wouldn't want to get in their way."

"What do you think, Rahym?" Nury looks at me, his innocent eyes wide. I know exactly why he's worried, too—Fatma's up there, and he wants to swoop in and be the hero. The problem is there are no heroes in our world.

But I do remember being in his shoes with Maysa when I was younger. And, perhaps, I understand his position in a different way now. I want to be up there as well, because I want to make sure that Jennet is protected. I know that she can take care of herself, but that doesn't keep me from having this sense of...*overprotectiveness* toward her.

I clench my jaw. "I think you'll get your chance, Nury. Later. But don't get in the way now."

Nury watches the woman who has captivated his attention and gives a slow nod. "I guess you're right."

I can tell a defeatist attitude when I see one, so I change tack, trying to make him feel more at ease. "They all have different powers, right? Fatma will know if there are any demonlings coming. And they can do things we can't."

"Yeah." He nods. "Fatma senses demonic presences. Kerem can heal injuries. Sena can hold back fire. And Jennet has the ability to transfer energy to one person."

"Together, they make their own Halos with Nakir," Rabia says gruffly. "I don't even know why we're here."

"To make sure they get there," Emre says, finally piping up. "Or are you doubting your own position within our group?"

She shakes her head. "No, sir. But I'm not here to be fodder for the demonlings. You know that."

He nods. "I do."

"Everyone else has their reasons, but..."

"I know, Rabia," Emre says gently, and I remember him saying that her family died at the Caspian Sea. Suddenly, I see a flash of myself five, maybe ten years into the future where the absence of Maysa and Beste has molded me into someone cold. Someone I don't recognize. And I don't want that to be me. I'm sure that Rabia hasn't always been someone who hardened her heart. But there's a madness about her that comes when you don't care for anyone, when you're just living out of habit.

Which I realize I've been doing for three years now.

Does she have her own voice that speaks to her, too, I wonder?

Even though I'm still convinced that this whole journey will end in our deaths—I'm suddenly glad for it. I feel alive in a way that I haven't in a long time. It's giving me purpose for however much longer I'll be living.

Maybe I should mark off *Survive*. I may have moved beyond that to something else.

Live.

At least, I feel tranquil that way until the demonlings attack. And everything goes to hell.

It starts with Fatma screaming.

CHAPTER 18

"They're coming!" Fatma screams. "They're coming! *Theyrecomigtheyrecomingtheyrecoming…*"

She sways on her horse, dangerously close to falling off, and Nury spurs ahead beside me to catch her—he won't make it in time, but who am I to stop him? Thankfully, Kerem steadies her, and he rears back to us, shouting, "Demonlings are coming!"

"How many?" Nakir asks her. "And from where?"

Fatma looks way too pale and terrified for it to be anything but a huge crowd of them. "Lots," she whispers. With a shaking hand, she points toward the horizon. Right in our path. It's like they know we're coming to the Watchtower.

Maybe Abaddon already knows we're coming.

I exchange a nervous glance with the angel, and he catches my meaning. "We need to go," he says, licking his lips. "*Now.*"

"Fatma can't ride like this," Jennet says, reaching out to touch a hand to the younger witch's forehead. "She can barely stay in her saddle as it is."

"We'll die if we stay here. Rahym!" he roars at me, and I find myself gulping at the wrath of the angel. "Where's the closest Door Stop?"

It's the second day of our hard ride into the desert, and we're nearing the furthest extent of my knowledge of this landscape. I shift to pull the map out of my saddlebags, unrolling it with a slight tremor to my own hands.

Don't lose yourself now.

The map, to my dismay, shows the closest one about a three-mile ride in the direction right where Fatma was pointing. What kind of range does she have? Maybe they are too far. And maybe we can make it before we cross paths with the demonlings.

Assuming they aren't out specifically looking for us. Fuck, wouldn't that be bad luck? I think of the demonling that glared at me last night when I put out the other one's head as a deterrent. Like he was promising vengeance for his fallen comrade.

Shit.

"We have to head three miles in that same direction," I say, and I can see the change in everyone's demeanor as they realize what that means. I just love being the bearer of bad news. Based on Fatma's own shudder that runs through her body, it's close enough to them that she doesn't like it.

A few of the Halos curse under their breaths, panic evident on their faces.

"Where's the second-closest Door Stop, then? One that's not toward those monsters?" Murat asks desperately, speaking up for the first time in a long time. Good man. Smart man. Maybe he'll have conserved enough energy to survive this.

Unlike the rest of us.

I shake my head, because that was the first thing I'd

looked at. "Too far. We'd all fall into Hibernation before we ever get there."

"Then we have to go toward the demonlings," Nakir says.

Murat blinks. "But—"

"If we're caught out in the open, we will all die," Nakir says through gritted teeth. "We have no choice."

"I'll take Fatma," Nury pipes up. Kerem opens his mouth to object—I see it, but he exchanges a glance with Jennet, an unspoken conversation happening between them, and he relents, helping the young witch change horses from hers to sitting behind Nury. She wraps her arms around his middle and buries her face into his back. His cheeks redden, and it's not from the heat of the sun. Kerem takes the reins of Fatma's horses and ties them to Nury's saddle.

"Now, *go*," Nakir orders without skipping a beat. He snaps his reins, and his horse spurs into a gallop. The rest of us follow suit, urging our horses to go forward.

"Go, Alion!" I cry, clacking the reins.

For once, he listens, streaking across the desert, reminding me why Akhal-Teke horses are legendary for their speed. He may have been a bit of a bastard earlier, but he's moving, and that's what I'm hoping for. And maybe, with his speed and the other horses running at the same pace, we'll be able to make it after all.

Fat chance.

"Telescope!" Nakir shouts, holding out his hand to me.

I lean to one side of my saddle, dig around in my saddle-bags, and pull out the telescope. I'm reminded just how expensive the damn thing is—and he wants to pass it off like a baton while riding our horses at this clip?

We're all kinds of insane, aren't we?

Yep. We wouldn't be here if we weren't. And with that thought in my mind, I grit my teeth and pass it to him. No problems there as Nakir grabs it from me and holds it up to his eye. He stands up in his stirrups to get a better look ahead of us, his angelic strength and balance keeping him in the saddle. Another moment and then he yells, "Go faster!"

How the hell can we possibly go faster when we're already at our horses' limits, when we're nearing our own limits of exhaustion? Jennet glances at Nakir, disbelief in her eyes, before she looks at me, as if looking for validation from me. As if asking if I agree.

Hey, you're the crazy one.

That's right. I guess it's up to me. Suddenly, *Survive* seems like an impossible item on my to-do list.

At that thought, I dig my heels into my mount as I snap the reins again, harder. He snorts unhappily but surges forward, ahead of our pack.

I hear the pounding of hooves behind me, telling me that the other Halos are following suit.

Desperation edges into my mind as I haven't seen the Door Stop yet. It should be in view, since it's fewer than three miles from us now. There's not a lot of landscape to obscure it. The terrain's messing with me. We round a corner that must have blended with the rest of the tanned dunes, because I see a semicircle of rocks ahead of us, the outcropping casting shade into a little circle below. The Door Stop. It's not as protected as the one from last night, more of a lean-to than a cave.

Some Door Stops are much more secluded than others. This falls into the other camp.

"Shit," I ground out. I'd been hoping for something far more...protected. Less exposed to the elements. At this Door Stop, we'd have to hope that they miss our position entirely, or they'll be able to see us if they have half a brain. We're kicking up a huge trail of sand leading straight to our Door

Stop. And then there's the fact that they can probably hear us. Or smell us.

How well can demonlings smell anyway?

I inhale the hot desert air deeply through my nose and nearly gag. Hopefully not enough to smell my own brand of aroma.

Rabia and her horse near me, and even from my position on Alion's back, I can feel the sand shifting underneath me.

"Rabia!" I shout in warning as I flail wildly, veering away from the ground as it splits and erupts underneath Alion's gallop. No, no, no, not now. Don't do this to us.

Rabia has time to meet my eyes before the very earth belches fire, spewing with hot bursts of flame. Her horse collapses underneath her with a shriek as she goes down with a cry herself.

I yank hard on the reins, and Alion rears back with his own neigh. The other Halos stop to look at us, but I wave them on. "Go! Get to the Door Stop!"

Nury nods and spurs forward, bringing Fatma and her riderless horse with him. Emre and Murat follow him, drawing their weapons as they do so. Are the demonlings that close?

Shit, shit, shit, shit.

I don't have time to deal with demonlings, the uncontrollable fires, an injured horse, and Rabia—all at the same time. And to make matters worse, the ground continues to split, following a zig-zagged line ahead of them.

Sena, Kerem, Jennet, and Nakir stay behind, their horses pawing at the ground, panting with the burst they just exerted. Sena reaches out a hand and sweeps it to the side. Farther ahead of us, I see that the fires ahead of the others are extinguished.

"I can't hold it for long," Sena says with gritted teeth. "Hurry!"

"Kerem!" Jennet shouts, commanding the male witch. He swings a leg over his horse and drops heavily to his feet. Still on its side and screaming from the fall, the horse eyes Sena, the white of its eyes showing as Kerem advances on it.

"I don't know if I have enough to heal them both," Kerem says, glancing up at Jennet, as if asking for permission. I grasp my reins in fear—he's asking for Jennet's energy. *No.*

She doesn't question it as she jumps down and advances to Kerem and Sena. "I've got you," she assures the male witch, with gritted teeth. A quick glance at Nakir and me. "Make sure to get us to the Door Stop." She knows that they don't have enough to heal Rabia and the horse and make it to safety.

The angel nods but anxiously glances over his shoulder at the horizon. I think the demonlings are close. He doesn't say it, but I know his meaning.

"Do what you have to," he says.

I know that Nakir is strong, but I don't trust Jennet's life in his hands. Glancing nervously at Sena, who's holding the fires at bay, I jump off Alion as Jennet grabs Kerem's shoulder. Her eyes close in concentration, the ripple of the muscle in her jaw showing how hard she is focusing. A purple glow encapsulates both her and Kerem, and he reaches forth toward the horse. A red power emits from his hands as he massages the injured beast's flank.

The animal froths at the mouth, trying to escape Kerem's hands, which only make his injuries worse. And they are bad, I see now that I'm closer. The horse is burned badly, its rear back leg twisted in an unnatural angle. It should be put down with that kind of a break. The scent of burned hair and flesh hits my nose, and I fight the urge to gag.

Rabia is trapped underneath the horse's weight, grimacing as she pushes the bulk of him off her.

"Calm down," Kerem tells her serenely. "I need to get the horse fixed."

Rabia shoots him a shocked look, and I recognize it—that he'd expend the energy healing the horse before healing her. But in her pain, what she doesn't realize that if they don't heal the horse, she's as good as stranded. We need all the available horses in riding order.

Sweat breaks on Kerem's brow, and it's not from the heat of the desert.

"How far out are the demonlings, Nakir?" Jennet asks, her eyes closed. Her hands on Kerem's shoulders start to shake.

Nakir has the telescope pointed on the horizon. "Just hurry."

Jennet's lips pull up in a grim smile. "That bad, huh? Kerem?" Jennet has always had a sense of humor even in the worst of times.

The big man grimaces for a moment. "Al…most…"

The horse huffs and gets to its feet, nearly trampling Rabia, Kerem, and Jennet in the process, it's so spooked. It neighs and attempts to rear back, but Nakir grabs the reins and hushes it quietly. I don't know what power the angel has over the horse, but the beast quiets down.

Lucky bastard. My hand holding Alion's reins starts to feel sweaty.

Meanwhile, Rabia lets out a strangled cry, and we all see why. Her pelvis is crushed, and there's no way she'll be able to move without her limbs being healed, too.

How much energy do the witches have left?

Kerem furrows his brow and reaches forward, bringing that red energy to Rabia's hips. She looks too pale, too white. She's going into shock from being crushed. Her eyes close, and then she goes completely limp.

I feel the sand shift beneath my feet.

"Sena," I whisper in warning, too afraid to move, too afraid to draw a full breath. If we move too much, it could cause the ground to open up faster. But if we don't move—

"I...I can't..." the older woman whimpers.

Kerem's gaze flicks to me just as Jennet gasps, her body giving out beneath her. She spent all her energy. She collapses into the dirt next to Kerem, unconscious, but her eyes wide open. Kerem's expression turns from curiosity to pure horror. There's a tremble to his hands as he draws back, meaning that he's fading too.

We're stuck out here.

"Nakir—!" I start, turning toward the angel, just as the shifting stops. Which is not a good sign.

Uh oh.

You're telling me.

Horses start screaming as the ground opens up around us, fires sprouting like weeds, the tops of the conflagration taller than even me. It starts to my right and spreads as the ground shatters around us. I jump away as the dirt crumbles beneath my feet, and the flames catch my trousers on fire.

No time or energy to put it out, because we're being surrounded by fire. I surge forward as the burning cracks in the ground zag their way to Jennet. *My* Jennet. I throw my body in front of hers, meaning to take the brunt of the blast, but Sena throws her hand out, and I feel a pop at my back as the air pressure changes, keeping the fire from us.

Sena's eyes are huge as she looks down at me. *"Run!"* she whispers hoarsely.

Before she, too, collapses, right off her horse. Nakir is there to catch her and throws her body over his own saddle. Not the best way to carry a person, but it will suffice.

"Get out!" the angel snaps at me.

Panic brings me to my feet again, and I take Jennet with me as the fires continue their path. Bright-hot agony hits my back and my legs at one point, and I have to grit my teeth against the pain.

Not enough time to hurt. Not enough time to get rid of fires.

Apparently, those should be numbers two and three on today's list. On top of saving Jennet any way possible.

My past refuses to allow me to let her die on me.

I sling her over Alion and pull myself up in the saddle, just as Nakir picks up both Kerem and Rabia, the former faring only slightly better because he's awake. The angel helps the male witch into his saddle and hits the rump of the animal, hard. The horse whinnies unhappily and gallops off in the distance.

Toward the Door Stop.

More fires erupt around us, and I keep looking around us, unsure if I should go or if I should help Nakir more. There's still Sena, Rabia, and their horses who have unconscious riders. At what point do I turn tail and run?

"Think you can make it to the Door Stop?" Nakir asks as he throws me the straps to Jennet's mount.

Thank god, I caught them without trouble. Jennet lays untethered to Alion, and she is so still. So defenseless.

Hold on to her, I tell myself, and it's my own thoughts that tell me that. *Hold on to her. Don't let her go.*

"Yes," I say with a nod, sounding more confident than I feel. "I've got her."

For now, at least. And I'll do everything I can to keep it that way.

Nakir easily mounts his big stallion, even while carrying both Rabia and Sena, and he still manages to grab the reins of their horses.

Show off.

Crazily, I smirk.

"Let's go," Nakir commands, not addressing my expression, and he snaps the reins. His bay surges forward, and I follow suit, heading toward the Door Stop. We just have to make it. Kerem's horse is ahead of us, nearly there.

Nearly there.

I completely forgot about the demonlings that are advancing on us. *Shit, shit, shit.*

This is why going into the Door to Hell is such a bad idea.

We're never going to make it.

CHAPTER 19

I t starts as a high-pitched shriek I can feel growing all the way down my spine. A demonling spotted us, and the other demonlings join in the eerie cry. Once again, the moon-like landscape has obscured them from our sight.

And there are a shit ton of them. *Hundreds*. If not a thousand. So many, their ruddy skin seems to blend together to create a sea of evil and death. I can't see them clearly—the telescope would help with that—but I can certainly smell them.

One stands at the front of the horde, and I'd bet the Lodge that it's the same demonling from last night. The one that glared at me as if promising to come back and kill me.

These fuckers are good at following through on their promises. And if they attack the Halos because of me...all because I dared a demonling to attack...

"Nakir!" I shout. Because what else am I supposed to do? What the fuck can I do against a horde this big? Hell, even the Door Stop won't keep us from harm. We'd be lucky if they didn't trample over it.

The angel sees the horde and doesn't hesitate as he draws Jan, the angel sword, from the scabbard on his back. It sings as it's freed.

Even though our lives are on the line, I can't help but stare at the beautiful weapon. It's been a few years since I've seen it—Nakir doesn't exactly take it out that often to show it off, and for good reason. In the scabbard, it's a spectacle. Outside of it, it's a thing of beauty.

It's about fifty-two inches of heavy Damascus steel gleaming in the sunlight. Ancient designs twist and run down its length, and the hilt and pommel shimmer with gold.

The thing must weigh a ton, but Nakir wields it like a butter knife.

Then, absurdly, he swings one leg over his horse's saddle and drops to the ground. Like he wants to take this horde on himself.

"Take them to the Door Stop," Nakir yells to me, slapping his horse's rump. The animal takes off, carrying Sena and Rabia with it. "Protect the others!"

I don't know what the hell I'm supposed to do against hundreds of demonlings. Especially when my own strength is fading and it's only about three in the afternoon. Even if I *could* keep them at bay, there's no way that I'll be able to protect myself until midnight.

No freaking way.

"Nakir—"

"*Just go!*" he shouts. He rushes forward, swinging the sword in an upward arc with one hand.

I'm paralyzed for a moment, watching him take on the horde. The demonlings must have noticed the lone man running toward them, because they surge forward like a blight racing through the landscape.

One angel against hundreds of demonlings. The odds are impossible.

And here I am, just a lowly man with a very important witch across my lap and two riderless horses that I somehow have to lead away from the clash and to safety.

What else am I supposed to do but run?

So I do.

I grit my teeth and kick my heels into Alion's side, willing the animal to run forward toward the Door Stop. Alion obeys, following Nakir's bigger horse, Sena and Rabia miraculously still on its back.

I feel Alion's gait slip underneath the pounding of his hooves, and we shift slightly.

Shit.

The ground doesn't even crack before it spews hot fire, blocking our way. Alion rears back with a scream, and I hang on for dear life.

And, because I'm a useless son of a bitch, I fall off with Jennet on top of me. The wind gets knocked out of me, and a groan escapes my lips as I roll onto my side.

Fucking bad luck.

I blink a few times as the two images swirling across my vision struggle to combine into one, and I wince as something gooey falls on my forehead. Then I see why. There's a damned demonling that has broken off from the rest of the group, and he grins over me, his drool dripping in thick globs. As my eyes focus on him, he holds up a bone to pound my skull in.

Definitely won't be able to mark off *Survive*.

Never thought it would go this way. Then again, I'm not sure what I expected. I always knew I was going to die in the Door to Hell. Just wish it were from a more...*pretty*...being. This demonling is so damn ugly.

The blow never comes.

Thick, hot blood sprays me in the face. Not mine. Too thick and black to be my own. A relieved whoosh escapes my lungs, the most I can manage at the moment.

The demonling blinks, as if in surprise, before its top half slides off its hips and legs with a wet squelch, and it collapses to the ground in two pieces.

Dead.

Murat steps over Jennet and me, wielding a sword with both hands. He gives a toss of his head toward the Door Stop. "Run," he says gruffly.

Somehow, I get to my feet, carrying Jennet with me. Murat's eyes flick to her before his face hardens. We share an unspoken agreement between us, that he'll buy us enough time to get to the Door Stop. He may not like me, but he cares enough for Jennet to save my ass, too.

Thank you.

Jennet's body feels so limp as I haul her over my shoulder, and her head dangles over my back. Alion keeps running in front of me, and I spot Nury emerging from the Door Stop to intercept him and keep him from continuing the run.

Emre runs toward us as well, carrying a duo of knives at the ready to stand next to Murat to meet the enemy head-on. Nakir stands even closer to the horde as they rush our group, facing them like a lone hero.

I have to help them.

"Nury! Take her!" I shout. The younger man catches Jennet as I hand her over to him. "Protect everyone here!"

"What are you going to do?" Nury asks, his eyes wild.

I draw my yataghan, which seems like such a small, inconsequential weapon against such a huge enemy. But it's all I've got.

"Just protect them," I mutter, turning back to Nakir and

the others. I use my thready energy to jog back to Emre's and Murat's sides. The old, hardened warrior glances at me and nods approvingly. I don't know why, but I grin.

I must have lost what was left of my mind somewhere in between the fall from my horse and all the fires opening up.

Are you so sure about that?

I'm never sure about anything these days.

Nakir widens his stance, holding out the incredibly heavy blade with only one hand. I have no idea how he's doing it, because my hands are so sweaty. I have to use both my hands to hold my light yataghan, otherwise, it'd slip out of a one-hand grip.

Ahead of us, the sea of demonlings surges our way, and...

Nakir slashes the sword once in an arc parallel to the ground, and the force from the strike catches the demonlings in the front of the wave across the middle. For a moment, the demonlings stop and sway before blood spurts from wounds across their middles. A hundred of them go down all at once.

The power of a fallen angel.

I've never seen Jan being used this way before. Hell, until this moment, I really thought it was more of a showy ceremonial piece, that when Nakir confronted Abaddon, he'd just flash him with it and that would be that. After all, it was too big. Or so I thought.

Why didn't he use this power before? Why didn't he use it to save Maysa and Beste?

I cry out at the thought, but everyone else is too stunned to take in what Nakir had just done. The humans facing the horde. The horde themselves. Even Nakir, who breathes heavily from exertion, but he's coiled up, ready for another attack.

The demonlings' hesitation is short-lived, however, and

they move forward in succession, this time glowing orange with elemental fire. More prepared this time. Ready to incinerate us.

Nakir sweeps again, bowling over another hundred or so in a spray of blood and gore. Screams and wails cut through the landscape, ugly sounds from ugly creatures.

"Nakir didn't even touch them," Murat says in amazement.

"Hope he can keep this up," Emre mutters, looking to our left. I follow his gaze, where I see some stragglers who think they're cleverer than the others that are headed our way. "Hope you're ready, too."

I swallow nervously. "Sure."

I'm not.

In the back of my mind, I'm trying to calculate how much strength I have left. Not a lot, and especially in the face of so many demonlings. Minutes maybe. Not enough to make a meaningful dent in the army coming up against us.

"We're going to die," Murat says hopelessly, echoing my own sentiments.

"Where's your sense of adventure?" Emre asks, giving him a wide grin.

Murat's frown deepens. "I think I've had plenty of adventure already."

There are no more heroic words as the enemy engages us, hitting Emre first, who hacks and slashes his way through them, like the battle-hardened warrior he is. Murat and I stand back to back, wielding our weapons in front of us.

These demonlings are cleverer than the others, because they stay back, throwing elemental spells our way, which causes Murat and me to dodge and split up. So much for having each other's backs. Even though I don't like Murat that much, I'd rather have him at my back than open air.

"My kingdom for a bow and arrow," I mutter before the Lodge flashes in my mind of what was left of "my kingdom." *They* did that. This asshole gaggle of demonlings.

Maysa.

Beste.

My life.

My purpose for being. Gone.

And now I see that Nakir had the power to stop it.

The rage blinds me again, and I scream as loudly as I can as I run and leap into the fray, hacking at anything that gets in my way. The rage is hot, and there's fire all around me, but I keep slashing and slicing.

They're why I'm facing the world alone. Why I'm broken and will never get the pieces put back together. I'm going to kill them. I'm going to kill all of them. I don't know how, without having magical powers or without an angel sword.

But I am going to destroy every last one.

Starting with these.

What have you been doing for the past three years?

I'm not going to let my inner voice shame me. Not when it's taken everything I have to not lose myself.

"Rahym!"

Through the din in my ears, I hear Murat's voice. Somehow, I managed to get far ahead of them, deep into the throng of demonlings, and I avert my attention back to them for a split second, seeing them running up to me, fighting their own demonlings along the way. The demonlings cast fire spells, and us humans' only defense is dodging their attacks.

I cough, choking on blood that isn't mine. I'm covered in it, and the realization tempers my anger because it's disgusting, and I wonder if the blood is in any way poisonous. I wipe it away with the back of my hand, the smell of the demonlings filling my nostrils.

Showers are scarce out here. If I survive this, I'm going to smell like demonling corpse for a long time.

"How many?" I pant as I whirl around. I hack my yataghan in empty air, as all of the enemy around me are dead. Did I do that?

I swallow thickly, hoping that it's saliva and not something else. "How many are left? How many demonlings are left?"

"Nakir—" Emre starts, and I follow where he's looking. I blink, confused, as the angel is standing by himself, piles of vanquished demonlings around him. He's covered in blood like I am, and the only part of him that's not covered in gore is his eyes. He glances back at us and flashes us the ghost of smile before his legs buckle beneath him and he collapses. The hero of the hour, reduced to being unable to hold himself up.

Welcome to life with the curse.

Murat sighs and combs his hand through his hair. "Well, shit. Who has the strength to drag him to the Door Stop?"

I let out a shuddering breath. "Not me," I whisper. The ground tilts beneath me, and it's not one of the fires sprouting from the earth. I'm staggering as my own hibernation takes over.

I fall face-first into the fine sand.

Hopefully there are no more demonlings out here. Because if there are, we're fucked.

CHAPTER 20

Like usual, my strength snaps back into my body, and I push myself up onto all fours, reaching for my weapon. Right on cue, my heart is pounding faster and faster, like it wants to abandon me and retreat back from the desert.

Because I'm still in the Door to Hell. Hell, I'm still right where I collapsed earlier. Were we that close to dying that no one could pull me to safety? Or were we just at that point all along?

My fingers find the yataghan, and I close them, feeling the ivory handle of the blade. It's gummy, as I hadn't had the chance to clean it before I succumbed to the hibernation.

I'm almost confused for a moment as I frown at the bodies surrounding me. It's dark outside, the middle of the night, and the only thing that gives away the bloody landscape around me is the moonlight glinting off their ruddy skin.

So many demonlings and pieces of demonlings. And they all smell so stinking bad.

Imagine if you had died along with them. You'd be spending an eternity with that stench.

I'd rather not imagine that, thank you very much. Because that is way too damn close to the truth. It's way too close to what *could* have happened out here.

"Rahym!"

I whirl at the voice, wildly wielding the yataghan in front of me. I don't trust much of what happens when I first wake up. Too many people try to take advantage of you, and well, *look* at where I just woke up.

Not exactly a nice comfy bed.

Jennet halts a few feet from me, holding up her hands placatingly. "Relax," she says softly. "It's just me."

I'm so battle-ready right now that it takes everything I have to loosen my grip on the blade and bring it down. I force myself to focus on her, on her face, and how she looks as bone-tired at me.

"What happened?" I ask. "What time is it?"

She regards me for a moment before sighing. "It's just after midnight." She crosses her arms in front of her body, putting up a physical barrier between us. That doesn't escape my notice, despite the fact that my mind is firing at a million miles a minute. "Everyone is waking up from their hibernation," she says almost sheepishly.

"Everyone?"

She lets out a shaky, self-deprecating laugh. "Yeah. It was close this time. Too close."

Too close indeed.

I glance around me, seeing Emre and Murat groaning as they start to stir. They had collapsed right alongside me, a testament to how close we were to losing this battle. Beyond us, I can dimly make out the shape of Nakir as he shakes off the effects of his hibernation. There's no joking, no joviality to waking up.

We're simply alive, when it was too close for comfort.

I lick my lips and look around. "So no one was awake until now?"

"No," Nury says, making his way out to us. His eyes are somber and sad as he casts his gaze down in shame. Why, I'm not sure. We're all alive right now; isn't that what counts? "I'm so sorry," he says softly. The night air is so still and quiet, I can hear him clearly. "I was at the Door Stop when I saw you guys fall. And I knew that I could make it out here and survive and protect Fatma and—"

"It's fine," Nakir says with a heavy sigh as he stalks his way back toward the Door Stop. "We're all alive now. You were protecting our most important, precious asset."

His eyes are on Jennet as he says that, and I feel something flare to life within my chest. Jealousy? Over calling Jennet precious?

Yes, that is exactly what you're feeling. Which is a damn sight better than feeling depressed.

Shit, I don't have the time or energy for jealousy. Especially since I know that Nakir is a fine specimen. If he suddenly decided that he wanted Jennet as his lover or wife or whatever it is that angels have with mortal women, then there's nothing I can do.

I'm just Rahym Tezel. Failed Lodge owner. Widow. Father to no one.

I suck in a shuddering breath as I push myself to my feet. "We're lucky we're not all dead," I snap at Nakir as I pass him. Jealousy, apparently, turns me into an asshole.

I like the taste of it in my mouth.

Nakir only chuckles. "Luck has everything to do with it."

"Don't be coy," I snap. "You have the lives of all of us in

your hands and you're treating this like some sort of daytime outing? Shall I get you some tea or something?"

The angel narrows his eyes at me before shaking his head. "What's gotten into you, Rahym?"

I throw up my hands, not understanding what's gotten into me, either. All I know is that we nearly *died* out here. Died, and for what? Some sort of misplaced sense of adventure? The belief that we are the ones destined to save the world?

I realize now that it's impossible. In the shadow of the Watchtower, which I can see smoldering in the distance, we're still so far, still tired, exhausted.

That goal seems impossible.

I'm a fool. Nakir is a fool. We're all fucking fools out here, because we're up against odds that are impossible. With the curse, we're at a huge disadvantage, and with all of the monsters roaming around the Door to Hell, we're fighting against a never-ending stream of shit.

And at the end of it all, we're no better than shit on the bottom of someone's boot. Abaddon's boot, most likely.

"Why was that the first time I saw you using Jan like that?" I snarl at Nakir, lashing out with the only thing I have that makes some sense. "Why haven't you used your sword like that before?"

Nakir gives me an incredulous look. "It hasn't been needed like that before. And it takes a lot out of me."

"You could have done that to save the other Halos." I grit my teeth. "You could have saved Maysa and Beste with it."

Understanding dawns across his face. "You were there," he reasons. "You saw what happened. There was no chance. I—"

I try to reason with my own mind. When I had last journeyed into the Door to Hell with Nakir, we hadn't been attacked with such a huge force as today. And we were headed back to the Lodge on the very last vestiges of our strength to warn them of the wildfires and get them out of there. I had collapsed only a few yards from my wife and child and heard them scream as the fire surrounded them and the rest of the Halos.

Somehow, I had been saved. And for what? So that I could die doing the same exact thing?

Luck.

Fuck luck and fuck everything to do with that. I want answers. I want my life back. I want something worth living for. And right now, the only thing that I can grasp with my panicked mind is that Nakir could have done something—anything—and he didn't.

I thrust my hand toward the Watchtower. "Why not zap your sword over to the Watchtower and slash it to bits? You seem to be pretty damn good at it."

I see the ripple of the muscle along his jaw, and the intensity heightens within him, burning at me. I refuse to budge.

"Rahym—" Emre says, reaching out for me. I shrug away from his grasp.

Nakir and I still hold each other's glare, and it could have been the two of us at that moment, for all I knew. "You know I did everything I could," he whispers. "I never would have—"

"Fuck you," I snarl as I storm toward the Door Stop. So much wasted energy on this conversation and my barely contained anger. But I don't care. Why care when all Nakir has to do is swing that sword? Why have the Halos at all?

I storm my way to the Door Stop, pushing past a stunned Jennet.

"Rahym!" she calls after me, but I ignore her. "*Rahym!*"

"Don't," I hear Nakir telling her. "He needs to grieve in his own way."

I don't want to admit that he's right. My eyes burn with something like tears, and I blink furiously to keep them at bay as I walk into the relative safety of the Door Stop. Nury, Fatma, and the others watch me with apprehension. Even Rabia, who grimaces and fights to sit up with her pelvic injuries, watches me warily as I head to the stone outcropping, away from the others. I'm sure they don't want to be around a half-crazed man any more than I want to be that half-crazed man.

I just want to feel happy again. And it won't ever happen again.

I curl up on the floor, facing the wall, and try everything I can to fall asleep. It takes all too long, and even sleep isn't restful.

I hate the Door to Hell.

FINGERTIPS BRUSH MY CHEEK, fluttering gently. I float on my dreams, trying to place the touch. Maysa used to wake me up like this. She'd feel the edges and curves of my face in order to commit my physique to memory. So many times, I woke up in bed with her just watching me as the pads of her fingers brushed my cheek.

I remember that those fingertips didn't have calluses, as Maysa never did get wizened and roughed up by the world around us. She'd work as hard as possible, but her skin remained soft. And her smile never faltered.

These fingers are callused, however.

It's not Maysa.

I open my eyes to find Jennet sitting next to me as I had been sleeping. She freezes as I look at her, as if she were embarrassed at being caught during the intimate act. Her expression is a little fearful as our gazes meet. Then she glances away from me as her hand leaves my skin, leaving me cold and shivering.

How could her touch do something like that to me?

"It's nearly sunrise," she whispers, nodding to the east. "We should get a move on."

Get a move on.

Right. How?

I sit up and look around the rest of the campsite as the Halos go about their duties, making sure the horses are stocked, gathering up everything. We didn't exactly make camp here, but we still clean up and try everything we can to hide our tracks.

Kerem is leaning over Rabia, and I see the power glowing in his palms as he continues to heal her wounds. She glares at him, like she wants to rip off his face. After all, he had saved her horse before saving her. I'm sure that does a lot for her self-confidence.

"I guess Alion will be happy," I mutter, combing a hand through my hair. "Another day of suicide missions. Maybe he'll run off when I die."

"Rahym." The hurt note in Jennet's voice makes me look at her again. Her expression is pinched, like she's in physical pain herself. She takes a breath and takes my hand in both of her own. "What happened out there? Between you and Nakir?"

"We nearly died," I say. "That's what."

"But we're still here." Our gazes meet, and she softens, smidge by smidge. "We're still fighting."

"For what?" I whisper. "Is the cost worth it?"

Jennet licks her lips as she mulls over her answer before she finally speaks. "Yes." She closes her eyes, as if pained.

ERIN HAYES & REBECCA HAMILTON

"It's worth it. Because if it keeps families together—if it keeps one man from losing himself to grief—then it's worth it. No one should ever feel powerless."

She's talking about you.

"And you believe that we won't feel powerless if we win?" I ask. Big *if* there, but I hold my breath, waiting for her answer.

She wets her lips again, averting her eyes. "Yes. I hate what the curse and the Door to Hell have done to you, Rahym. I know...I know I left before anything could have changed between us, but...you have to keep fighting."

"Why?"

"Because..." Her lips catch mine, soft and supple against my unyielding mouth. I freeze against the contact, my eyes widening as I take in everything that's happening in this very moment. Jennet, my friend from childhood, whom I haven't seen in nearly two decades, is kissing me. Mouth-to-mouth resuscitation in a very emotional way. She's trying to will me back to life.

If I'm completely honest with myself, then I would acknowledge that my chest is swelling with something like...*hope*...

And it's all because of her.

I don't move. I *can't* move. Because the last person to kiss me like this and put her trust in me died. And there's no way I can put Jennet through that. Hell, there's no way I'd survive that.

She pulls back. "There are always reasons to keep fighting."

I can't say anything. I don't move. I just watch her, stunned.

A pained expression crosses her beautiful features as she

gives herself a quick nod, as if she's shaking off the moment and burying it in the sand of this Door Stop.

But it did happen. And I don't know what to make of it. We *can't* be anything more, because that makes both of us liabilities. That would ruin Maysa's and Beste's memories. And if everything crumbled around me and I lost myself, it would ruin me from the inside out.

And that's something I can't handle.

Jennet takes it in an entirely different way, though. She nods and gets to her feet. "Don't give up, Rahym," she warns me. "Don't you dare give up."

She walks away, leaving me alone. I groan and comb a hand through my hair, realizing that I still have dried demonling blood on me. Jennet had kissed me even though I'm at my dirtiest, smelliest worst.

Maybe we're all losing our minds out here.

Nakir is getting his horse ready, and he's watching me intently. I'll have to face Nakir sooner or later. But right now, I just can't.

Not with a desert of emotions and mine fields between us. I...*can't*...

I get to my feet and walk over to Alion, who regards me with one wide eye.

"Don't you judge me either," I groan to my horse.

Alion responds by lifting up his tail and pissing all over the ground, including my boot. Great. Now I'm covered in demonling blood *and* horse piss. If this isn't Hell, then I don't know what is.

CHAPTER 21

The day goes by relatively uneventfully. We just ride our horses as the sun beats down on us, moving from one horizon to the other. We take turns, having one person on watch, while the rest of us are tied to our saddles, ready to be alert at a moment's notice. Even Rabia, with her injuries from the night before, is quiet, and she doesn't snap at anyone.

We don't cross paths with any more demonlings as we travel across the hot, sandy desert. No more wildfires sprout.

Small blessings.

I remain quiet, lost in my own thoughts as I steer Alion at the back of our group. He is decidedly an asshole today. Pissing all over my feet was just the start of him doing everything possible to let me know that he's unhappy with the status quo.

"You and me both, horse," I mutter, unimpressed.

Ahead of me, Nakir looks back at me, as I'm the first one to have spoken in a while. I glare back defiantly at him, still smarting from the night before, as he swivels around in his saddle to face front again. He clacks his reins, and his horse moves ahead.

I guess I'm just like Alion today. I'm not in the mood for anyone's shit or sympathy or what the hell else you have in the desert like this.

But Nury hangs back, the innocent bastard, and falls into step beside me. "What was it like?" he asks. "Being a miner out here?"

I frown at him, not really following what he's saying. "What do you mean?" I attempt to wet my lips with my dry tongue. "It was exactly like working in Hell."

Nury nods. "Yes, but…" His eyes sweep the dunes and hills around us, his expression wavering between suspicion, worry, and terror.

Ah, so that's why he's asking. The poor man is frightened out of his mind.

Well, aren't you as well?

No, I have zero fucks left to give.

You know that's not true. Why would you be so concerned for Jennet's wellbeing, then?

I have no answer for that. And I realize that Nury has been patiently waiting for me to answer him, to give more insight into the lives of the men who'd risk themselves for money.

"Some days were better than others," I say finally. "Mining natural gas has always been dangerous work, and our bosses knew that. You didn't always have to work within the Door to Hell in order to get paid. So many days were spent with deliveries, recuperating, and being around those you cared about." I snicker. "Come to think of it, they must have done that to keep us coming back. You always knew *why* you faced Hell."

"Did you always have to deal with demonlings?"

145

I snort. "How else do you think I knew to hack off that demonling's head and stick it outside the Door Stop?" Nury flinches but doesn't respond, and I chuckle mirthlessly. "Yeah, I had to deal with them every time I went into the Door. They were always a constant threat."

"Did they...hurt anyone?"

I know that Nury doesn't mean anything by it, but I have to press my lips together and inhale slowly before I answer. "All the time. So many miners died out here." I imagine their bones underneath the very ground we're walking on, the flesh blown away by the endless hot winds and sand. I lost so many friends and colleagues out here.

I'm sure I lost parts of myself, too. I haven't been innocent for a long time.

"Why'd they stop production?" Nury asks, his voice breaking into my thoughts. It's only been about ten years since they had to stop, when I was around his age myself, but I guess if no one ever talked about it, then we'd all forget, wouldn't we?

Has it really only been ten years since we lost electricity?

"As the natural gas dried up near the edges of civilization, we had to venture farther and farther into the Door in order to drill for more gas. By that point, it got too dangerous, so they were forced to close down the mine."

"Too dangerous."

My entire body stiffens at the memories. "Yeah," I say. "We were attacked after venturing too far. When our horses were killed, the wildfires started, and none of us could outrun it with the curse and everything. And...I was the only survivor of my group." I nod toward Nakir at the front of our group. "It's why he approached me in the first place. I know the Door to Hell better than anyone alive."

Nury blanches. "So you're——"

I nod. "The sole survivor of my mining team." I've spent my life wondering why I was the only one to survive.

"I'm so sorry," he says honestly.

"Yes," I murmur softly. "Me too." I don't deserve anyone's sympathy for that. I was the lucky one. The one who made it back to tell so many widows, widowers, and families that their loved ones died. I made it back. Barely.

"And that's before you opened the Lodge?" Nury asks, as if trying to steer the conversation back to something more palatable for the innocent.

I even chuckle at it. If he only knew that what happened at the Lodge afterward was worse. "I had originally become a miner to raise a dowry so I could marry Maysa," I say softly. "Her father owned the Lodge before us, and there was never anyone good enough for her. So that's why I took on such risky work. To earn approval in her father's eyes."

"And when they shut down the mine?"

"Well," I say slowly, sifting through so many memories, "they gave me a large payout for being the only survivor. So I was able to impress Maysa's father with it, and he allowed us to be married. None of us knew he was sick at that point." My fingers tighten on Alion's reins. "He died a year to the day after Maysa and I were married."

"I'm sorry," he says again.

"Don't be." Mainly because I have no idea how he could have done anything different about it. "It is what it is. It brought Maysa and me together."

"And Jennet? How did you know Jennet before this?"

I look ahead at the witch who is talking in hushed whispers to her fellow witches. "She was my first love," I murmur so softly, I doubt he can hear. I clear my throat, speaking a little louder with my next words. "The three of us grew up together. Maysa's father ran the Lodge, and

Jennet's parents worked with mine for delivering supplies. So...we were the kids of colleagues, and while we were forced together, it ended up all right. Jennet was always the more adventurous of us. Maysa was gentler. And I was just along for the ride."

I stroke the side of my jaw, feeling the stubble growing there. I remember the feel of Jennet's lips against me, both as of this morning and from many years before. Jennet was my first kiss. Maysa was the one to have my heart.

And now, with all that's been lost between us, I don't know what to make of it.

"What happened between you and Jennet?" Nury asks.

Ah, so he did hear that part.

I snicker. "After her dad died, she disappeared. And I had no idea why or where she went to. Turns out, it was to become a witch." I gesture toward her. "Up until a few days ago, I thought she had died."

"Fatma told me about what it's like to be a witch," the younger man says, glancing up at the pack at the front. "They take you away from your tribe and assimilate you into theirs. It's hard and—"

I nod. "I think that's from centuries of being persecuted based on their beliefs."

"But now, they could save us all."

I catch Jennet's gaze again, and her eyes crinkle at the corners as she gives me a small smile. A smile that's meant for just me, one that we've shared since we were kids. I hadn't realized that she felt that way still.

"Yes," I whisper. "Yes, they could save us."

Suddenly, Alion knickers and rears back, nearly toppling me off his back. Nury's horse follows suit and cries. Unlike me, Nury falls off, landing in a heap on the ground as his horse runs back the way we came. In this environment, with everything at stake, we can consider the beast to be gone for good.

Shit. Fucking shit!

When the insane part of your mind comes unglued, you've really lost it.

The other horses are going crazy as well. I grit my teeth and look at the horizon.

"What is it?" Murat asks, his voice shrill. "What's happening?"

Jennet cuts her questioning gaze over to Fatma, who shakes her head wildly as she attempts to control her horse. "No demonlings nearby! I don't sense anything."

No, this isn't from demonlings. I know how horses act around them, and this is something different. Like they're spooked from something bigger. I recognize it from an incident long ago when I was a miner. We barely made it to a Door Stop in time to save ourselves.

No. No. Please don't let it be that.

The scent of fire and embers on the wind catches my nose, confirming what my eyes haven't yet.

I tug on the reins and gallop forward to the edge of a hill to see for myself. I don't have to get far, because as I round the top, I see the swirling masses of dark clouds rising from the desert into multiple tornadoes. Orange, red, and every color in between billows out from the cyclones, launching embers and fires out into the air to add to the chaos. Lightning crackles above from the friction the swirls are creating.

A firestorm. Rapidly ripping through the Door to Hell, like a demonling's teeth tearing flesh from limb.

No wonder we haven't see any demonlings. Those that we didn't kill last night have been fried to a crisp.

We're too far from a Door Stop, and I don't even know if one would be enough to protect us from this deadly storm.

It's moving too fast. Hell, we didn't even smell it until now because it's moving so quickly.

So much for having an easier day.

I have to fight to maintain control of Alion as he tries to buck me off and run away from the storm. I know it's futile, though. There's nowhere we can run right now to get away from it. This firestorm will consume *everything*.

"What's happening?" Nakir asks as he pulls up right beside me. I twist my head, glaring at him. The angel pales as he faces the maelstrom that's heading our way.

His expression is the same as mine: we're doomed.

"Can you use your sword to cut through the storm like you did last night?" I snap at him. "Or is that something you're waiting to reveal to your third group of Halos?"

Nakir's eyes narrow at me in a challenge. "Is there nowhere nearby?"

"Only choices are where you'd like to be cremated. Don't think anyone will be coming to our funerals, though."

Yeah, you've fucking lost it.

The angel huffs a breath. "Sena!" he roars, turning around in his saddle. "*Sena!*"

At first, I want to yell at him that there's no hope, but Sena streams past us on her mount, her wizened face set and determined. She waves her arm, yelling, "Everyone, come with me!"

But that's *toward* the fiery inferno that's headed our way. Which is more insane than me.

My mouth hangs open, the retort dead on my lips, as a second person joins her on this crazy charade.

Jennet.

The two witches run by Nakir and me, confronting the storm in what can only be called a suicide mission. What the hell are they supposed to do? I know that Sena's power lies in her ability to keep fire at bay, but this is something else entirely.

This is madness.

Nakir gives me one more glance before heading off and following them. Everyone else has recovered from this crazy request, and they're following in line. Like a bunch of lambs off to the slaughterhouse. Because that's what going to happen.

The worst part is that there's nothing I can do to protect Jennet. I'd been willing to throw everything away yesterday when I confronted the demonlings. But there had been the hope that we would somehow survive.

We won't survive this.

"Rahym!" Emre shouts as he passes me. Nury is riding behind him, as his horse has run off. "Come on!"

"*Where?*" I shout. "Where!"

Alion neighs unhappily as I follow everyone else, the last of our group to head out to a flat space that's out in the open. We're going to die. We're going to be caught up in this and die, charred to a crisp.

"Tether your horses!" Nakir yells as he dismounts.

Tether them *where*? How? What the hell are we doing out there? We could be running away. But it seems like there's nowhere that's safe.

Big hands pull me off Alion as Emre takes a bandana and puts it over the horse's eyes to keep him from seeing the fires around us. Dazedly, I watch as the others follow suit, covering their horses' eyes and tethering them to fossilized husk of a tree that looks like it would crumble apart with any amount of pressure. If the horses want to get away, it won't take much.

Luckily, they seem too spooked to be anything but docile.

But when my eyes fall on Sena and Jennet, everything else

151

leaves me. I watch as the older witch stalks out to the edge of our little throng, and when she finds a spot, she kneels, gripping the sand within her clenched fists.

Jennet takes a spot next to her, gently putting a hand on Sena's shoulder. There are a few words that are exchanged between the two of them, but I can't hear it over the roar of the wildfires headed our way.

Are they attempting to hold the fire at bay? How? When we're trying to battle a force of nature with rapidly depleting energy, we're helpless.

"Rahym!" Nakir shouts. "Help us!"

I have to wrench my gaze away from what's happening to look at him. For once, the angel looks frightened, as if this hadn't been imagined in all his bravado and talk of being heroes and saving the world. *No*, I want to tell him. *This is what our reality truly is.*

I make my way over to the rest of the group, huddled by the horses.

"Hold this," Nakir shouts as the roar grows around us. "Make sure we don't lose any more horses!"

We're about to die and he's worried about losing the horses. The absurdity of it almost makes me laugh hysterically. The only thing keeping me from losing it is my worry about what's happening to Jennet.

"What about—?" I turn to look at the two witches standing several yards in front of us, as if they're our last beacon of hope. Impossible. There's no way they can stop this. They seem like two fragile leaves about to blow away in the hot wind.

I lift my gaze up just in time to see the firestorm descend upon us, hitting the two of them first. I open my mouth to yell at Jennet to—what, exactly, I don't even know—but the fire sucks all the oxygen out of my mouth, and my tongue burns along with the rest of me.

Someone's screaming.

The horses are screaming and trying to pull away.

I'm screaming. And my eyes are squeezed shut as we're all barbecued alive.

But death doesn't come to me like I thought it would. Taking a tentative, shaky breath, I open my eyes.

We're in the eye of the firestorm, in a kind of protective bubble that's keeping the flames at bay. I watch as the fires swirl around us, unbearably hot. The thunder from the storm roars around us, splitting our eardrums and giving me this hollow feeling as my heart pounds in my chest.

We're alive, somehow. And I see why.

Sena and Jennet take the brunt of it, their two forms shrouded in smoke and eye-watering ash. Sena's yelling, her arms and legs buckling underneath her with exertion. I know she's powerful and this is her specialty, but I doubt she's combated fire like this. Jennet seems to attempt at shielding her with her body, but she's struggling to stay upright herself.

How long do they have against the storm? How big is the storm?

They're not going to hold out.

I don't know what I'm doing, but my muscles move of their own accord.

"Nury!" I shout, and I thrust the reins into the other man's hands. "Take Alion!"

I don't wait for a verbal answer, but Nury's fingers close around mine. His eyes are too wide, his skin too pallid. Like the rest of us. We're powerless in the face of such tremendous power.

I may be powerless. I may just be a human and get in the

way. But I know that if I don't do anything, we're going to die anyway. Might as well see if there's *anything* I can do.

In a low crouch, I make my way to Jennet and Sena. Sena's too lost in her own battle of pain and will, but Jennet's eyes flick to me, questioning, *begging* me to go back with the others. "Rahym, you need to—"

"Can you take my strength?" I yell above the roar, cutting her off.

"What?"

"You can give someone your strength. Can you take mine and give it to Sena as well?"

She blinks. "I've never tri—"

I cup her cheek as she looks at me, her bottom lip trembling. Despite the death and destruction around us, she's never looked as beautiful as she does right now when she truly believes that these may be our last moments together. "Take mine," I say so that only she can hear. "*Try.*"

Her eyes flutter closed, and at first, I don't feel anything other than the heat and the roar of the storm.

"I'm sorry," she whispers suddenly.

I cry out in pain as it feels like my insides are being scooped out of me with a huge spoon, and I nearly crumble under the weakness that comes over me. Whenever I fall into hibernation, it's a quick, gradual sensation without pain, but this is different. It feels like my very essence, what makes me *me* is being siphoned out of me.

I didn't know what to expect. But this is something else entirely.

It takes all my mental energy to stay upright, and through my haze of pain, I see that Jennet's eyes are open again, tears streaming down her face. I smirk, trying to remember what it was like when we were kids trying to battle the curse with playtime and stories.

With my thumb, I wipe away one tear. A shuddering breath escapes my lips, as I feel my reserves being nearly depleted. Jennet pulls away from me, breaking our contact, and a gasp of air fills my lungs as the feeling of being sucked out through my marrow stops. She turns back to the firestorm, her jaw set as she watches the storm.

I'm about to yell at the others to come over here and help, but both Sena and Jennet cry out at the same time. They both collapse to the ground, and I watch as the fire bursts through the protective barrier, first setting Sena alight, then snaking its way over to Jennet.

I try to stay awake, to pull them back from the brink.

But Jennet has taken most of my energy, and I stumble face first into the dirt.

You've failed.

CHAPTER 22

"—Hym. *Rahym.*"

There's a slap to my cheek. I guess whoever trying to wake me finally lost their patience.

I grimace and fight the person leaning over me. Aches explode all over my body in gauzy waves that I can't quite process. It's like I'm not currently in pain, but my body remembers it, and consciousness only brings it back into full light.

I don't want to wake up. Because even if I'm not in agony, there's one kind of pain that I don't know if I can witness and survive.

Jennet. Please don't be dead.

Both my subconscious and I seem to be on the same page as far as that. Jennet's been one of the best parts of my life for past few days—hell, for my entire life—and I've only just reconnected with her only to fail her in her time of need.

I don't want to wake up, because I know if I lost Jennet, I'd lose everything. Just when I was getting my footing back after everything that's happened.

"Rahym, you need to wake up."

It's a man's voice, and I grimace as I open my eyes. It's Kerem, his stony face still as he regards me. There's a sadness to his expression, like he's afraid of me asking too many questions. I've had someone look at me like that before.

It was when I woke up after Maysa and Beste died.

No. No, it can't be true.

My throat closes as I regard him silently, waiting for him to say something.

He sighs and sits back, wiping a hand through his hair that's slick with sweat, like he's been exerting himself. He healed me, which explains why I'm having dull aches instead of pain. I try to sit up but feel every part of me stretch and pull in weird ways. My clothes are singed and smell of burnt *something*.

"Finally," Kerem mutters, more to himself than me. He turns away. "Nakir—he's awake."

I grimace as I finally pull myself into a sitting position. It's nighttime, which means that we survived the firestorm and that our strength is replenished again.

We're alive. My breath catches in my chest at the realization that it worked. We somehow came out of this crazy thing alive. Between the demonling attack and the wildfire, we're at the end of our reserves, strength, and wit.

But we're getting there. Maybe Nakir had been right this time. Maybe we have everything we need to get to the Watchtower.

We're at a Door Stop, one of the more secure, cave-like ones. Thank God for small favors, because after today's events, I don't think we could handle being exposed like our last Door Stop. It's large enough that the horses—what remains of them—are tied up in one corner. I look among them and count only seven—some of the horses must have either run or perished in the firestorm, and my heart sinks and breaks at the thought.

But Alion's among the ones that remain. I didn't realize until now how much I'd miss the bastard if he up and left me.

A campfire throws light and shadows throughout the Door Stop, giving both the illusion of warmth and doom. Like we're safe so long as we stay within the firelight.

There's movement from the other side of the fire. Nakir comes into view, his expression both relieved and exhausted. He exchanges a glance with Kerem, and the big man moves away from us, leaving the angel and me alone.

"You scared us back there, you asshole," Nakir murmurs.

The words actually make me smile. "Glad to see that your sense of humor didn't burn either," I say blithely.

He chuckles darkly before sighing. "Thank you."

"For what?"

"For being a crazy son of a bitch who puts others before himself. If you hadn't pulled that stunt, I don't think…" He swallows self-consciously before giving himself a shake. "Well, I think we all would have died."

I caught his hesitation, though, and I swallow thickly. "How are Jennet and Sena?"

More hesitation from him. More lies, even if he's trying to protect my feelings.

I try to scramble to my feet, but Nakir catches my arm. His angel strength keeps me from moving, and I whirl on him. "What. The. Fuck. Happened?" I growl at him.

The corners of Nakir's eyes crinkle a little. "Sena's power gave out before the wildfire passed over us. And—" He swallows thickly. "And Sena didn't make it."

It takes a moment for that to sink in. "But how?" I fumble for words, trying to piece together a question that will give me clarity. Sena can't be dead. She was just using her power to save all of us.

Nakir sighs and sits back, rubbing his face with his hands. "Sena's power gave out just before the storm passed. She was burned—badly—before Kerem had a chance to get to her. She died before he could heal her."

I shake my head. "No," I whisper. "No."

Jennet.

Jennet had been right next to Sena when that happened. Maybe a step back, but if Sena been set on fire by the storm...

I grab Nakir roughly by the collar. "Where's Jennet?" I snarl in his face. "Jennet—where is she? Is she—is she...?"

I can't even bring myself to say it. Nakir meets my eyes, and for a horrible moment as he opens his mouth, I think he's about to say the words that I realize frighten me more than a horde of demonlings or a wildfire.

"She's alive."

I blink furiously, trying to confirm that I heard what I thought I heard and not that it was what I *wanted* to hear.

"She's alive," Nakir repeats again, putting his big hand over my hand that's grappling him by the shirt. "She was injured in the fire, but Kerem was able to heal her. And you, actually."

Something akin to joy soars in my chest, and I try to look around Nakir to get a glimpse of Jennet. "So she's..."

"She hasn't woken up yet," he says quickly. "Kerem thinks she used up too much of herself in trying to transfer your energy to Sena."

I look at Kerem, who has been standing off to the side, watching me wearily. The healer witch sighs, seeming like he's too tired to do much. Even though it's not long after midnight, he must have used up a lot of his energy healing us.

"When is she going to wake up?" I croak.

Kerem lifts a shoulder, averting his eyes. "I don't know. When she wants to?"

I peer around the fire now, trying to get a glimpse of Jennet's sleeping form, now that I know she's not awake with the others. I find her next to Fatma and Nury, who hold vigil over her unconscious body. Nury has an arm over Fatma's shoulders, and the witch looks like she's been crying nonstop. Beyond them, Rabia, Murat, and Emre look shell-shocked, their own gazes watching the campfire.

We all look the worse for wear.

"I'm sorry, by the way," Kerem says softly. I turn back to him, in shock. "I spent most of my energy healing Jennet, so when I got to you, I—"

I shake my head. "No, it's fine. You did right."

Because the thought of Jennet in pain is enough to send searing pain throughout my entire body. She's resting at least now, though. If she wakes up—*when* she wakes up, she'll have to deal with the horrible news of Sena's death.

"You did right," I repeat.

I move toward Jennet's form. Neither Kerem nor Nakir call after me. I crawl to the side opposite of Nury and Fatma. Nury watches me as Fatma cries, lost in her own grief.

There's still hope. There's still something worth fighting for.

"Yes," I murmur to no one in particular as I reach out and take Jennet's limp hand, giving it a squeeze. "I'm just now realizing that."

WITH JENNET UNCONSCIOUS, Sena's death hanging heavily

over our heads, and the morale of the Halos at a dispirited low, we stay at the Door Stop for a few days to recuperate and figure out our next move. We don't speak to each other that much over this time, and the mood is somber at best. It just seems like we're all dealing with this in our own way.

We bury Sena just outside the Door Stop. Kerem wrapped her body up in one of the rugs we brought along for camp. It's not the biggest or the best funeral, and there are only a few words that are exchanged, but I feel like she'd understand. I didn't know Sena that well, but she seemed like a practical woman.

She'd understand. I'm sure of it.

It breaks my heart that Jennet isn't awake to say good-bye. And she remains unconscious, dead to the world without a way for me to reach her.

I rarely leave Jennet's side during this time, because I'm too afraid of her waking up without me. I don't want her to be alone when she finds out what happened to Sena.

Sena's death has rocked all of us to our cores, especially for Fatma and Kerem. As witches, they were closer than the rest of us to the older woman. I catch them exchanging a few words of condolences and grief to each other. Fatma has Nury to lean on for support, and I can tell that they have grown closer over these few days, including a few times when Fatma has come back to the Door Stop with her hair mussed.

Grief apparently brings people together. I understand that.

Kerem, however, has retreated further into himself. He heals the rest of my wounds the day after I wake up, but other than that, he's just existing at this point.

I want to tell him that it's not his fault. Sena didn't die because he didn't make it to her—she died because of the curse. But I know that he won't listen to me. I see his stubbornness reflected within myself. It's why I haven't left Jennet.

Rabia, Emre, and Murat seem to be the only ones who are existing with any sense of purpose. They're the ones who have less to lose. They're the ones who have lost the least in the past few days.

I'm almost jealous. We're doing all this for a greater purpose, but yet it's easier for those who don't have the deeper ties to everyone.

Nakir takes it harder than anyone, though. I know him well enough to see the tension in his jaw, the way he glances at everyone, the responsibility and the apologies that are sitting just on the tip of his tongue.

He blames himself. And I know I blamed him at the start of all this, and possibly it could be considered his fault…

But I don't pin it on him. I can't. I see the guilt in his eyes every time he looks at us Halos. No longer is he the powerful fallen angel. He's doubting himself, and it makes him appear…*human*. Which is something I never thought Nakir could ever be mistaken for.

And as for me? Our furlough gives me time to reflect on everything that has happened. My inner subconscious has been oddly quiet, too, until it's just truly Jennet and me sitting here.

"Wake up," I murmur to her. *Wake up.*

Jennet's chest only rises and falls, as she's lost in her own world. I look over at Kerem, who's sitting across the Door Stop. His face is grave as he turns away. His unspoken words are enough. He doesn't know why she hasn't opened her eyes yet.

I gulp back the lump in my throat and squeeze Jennet's hand. I hate how lifeless her fingers feel in my own, and I try to rub life into them, willing them to squeeze back.

She doesn't.

"I was the world's luckiest kid, you know," I whisper to her, hoping that my voice can act as a beacon for her. She doesn't stir, but I keep speaking, rambling really. It's a one-sided conversation similar to all the others I've had with her for days now, and every time, I get a little deeper in my own mind and what's been wrong with me.

It's as therapeutic for me as it is for her. Or at least that's what I tell myself.

"I don't know what I did to deserve you and Maysa," I say with a laugh, "but you two were always the highlights in my life. My best friends. And I knew back then that I could love you two. Maysa has my heart in one way, but you…you were the first. And in an entirely different way."

My throat closes up, and I swallow thickly to try to stem my own rising hysteria. "They always say that there's one soulmate for a person. And when Maysa and Beste died, I thought, 'That's it. There's nothing left for me in this world.' It felt that way, too."

I close my eyes and give myself a small shake. "I tried killing myself, you know. Back then, I couldn't imagine a world without Maysa and Beste, because they were my world."

It's a part of me that I've kept buried, that I'm afraid to admit or even remember. Because there was a point a week after I put Maysa and Beste into the ground where I couldn't stand to look at myself in the mirror anymore. I took one of Beste's toys, a ribbon on a stick that she played with in the garden, her twirls and jumps always entertaining to watch. I went to my quarters in the Lodge, where I spent the best nights of my life with my wife and some uncomfortable times with my daughter when she had nightmares. Even now, I would give anything to have those memories back.

163

I couldn't see beyond my misery, which is why I tied one of the ribbon around a branch of Maysa's tree and another end around my neck, and...

And...

And...

Yusup found me dangling and turning blue. I hadn't broken my neck when I jumped—yet another thing I couldn't do right—and he pulled me down, all while yelling at my staff to come help me. Afterwards, we didn't speak of what I tried to do. It was in the past, and I tried to push it as far back into the recesses of my mind as I could.

I threw myself into my work at the Lodge, because it was all I had left. The voice in my head came not long after that, as a way of keeping me company, the voice of reason to every impulsive urge I had.

I kept lists, because when you have something planned out for you, you have to keep to it. Because when you couldn't see beyond your pain, you could always go down to the next number and find some purpose. Even if it was just cleaning out the outhouse.

I rub at the spot on my neck where I nearly hanged myself. "I almost succeeded at it. At killing myself," I clarify, realizing that I had just spent a few minutes reflecting on my past. I wet my lips. "And I didn't die. For some reason, I didn't die. And I felt dead inside until I saw you."

She still doesn't stir, and I close my eyes. "When you left —when we were kids—I thought that was the worst thing to ever happen to me. You were here, and suddenly you weren't. I didn't know what had happened to you, and neither did Maysa. And I think that was when we moved from being friends to something more."

I pause, chewing on the inside of my cheek. "Your absence brought us together, Jennet. And right now, your absence is tearing the Halos apart. We need you." I squeeze her hand again. "*I* need you."

Nothing from her. I remember in old novels and movies that this is the part where the protagonist is supposed to wake up. And Jennet is still unconscious.

"Rahym?"

I look up to see Nakir standing over me, ill at ease. He seems like he doesn't want to disturb us, yet at the same time, he looks like there's something he wants to get off his chest.

"Yes?" I ask.

"Can we talk?"

I look down at Jennet and steel myself before finally nodding. "Of course."

Why not? It'll just take you away from her.

Nakir leads me outside of the Door Stop into the bright noon sun. I squint my eyes, looking around for any sign of dust trails of demonlings or more firestorms tearing through the desert. So far so good.

If there is any silver lining to be found in the wildfires, it's that the storm had killed off demonlings for miles around us.

I blink at the Watchtower, still in the distance yet seeming like we've inched ever so closer to the structure. We're the closest anyone has ever been to the tower. We're the closest ever to succeeding. And Abaddon's tower may as well be on a different planet.

"I wanted to say sorry," Nakir says by way of introduction.

"Sorry? For what?"

"For…" The angel gestures helplessly toward the tower, the dark obsidian structure obviously weighing on his mind. "*Everything*," he finally says.

I sigh, feeling the pull at my chest. "It's all right."

"No, it's not all right," Nakir says. "You have every right

to be mad at me, to hate me. Especially after everything that's happened. If you had been there for Maysa and Beste. If I had just hacked my way through." He clears his throat and gives me a hard look. "You have every right to kill me right now."

You have every right to make your own decisions.

I smirk, and Nakir gives me an incredulous look. Obviously, I just had part of this conversation in my head, so I wave off Nakir's comments. "I've been thinking about that," I say softly.

Nakir hesitates. "Yeah?"

"I was angry the other day," I reason, and he visibly pales. "You seem to be this all-powerful being with no scruples. You're stronger than any man, more magical than any witch, just a hell of a lot of *more*. And when I saw you do the impossible and kill that horde of demonlings, I thought you could do anything. Anything, and yet you didn't save Maysa or Beste."

"I couldn't—"

I hold up a hand to shush him. "I know that now. Believe it. You wouldn't have let Sena die if you were all-powerful. And you would have stopped Abaddon a long time ago. I get that, too. It's just…I know you're not human. Now I know what else you *aren't*."

Nakir lets my words sink in, and he gives a self-deprecating chuckle. "Yes," he whispers. "I used to think I was superior to you humans. Back with the first Halos, I thought that with an angel on your side, anything was possible. And that arrogance…ended us."

"You have another shot," I tell him. "Use it wisely."

He scoffs slightly, shaking his head. "When I get to Abaddon…"

"When *we*," I point out. "Because you apparently need

some witches and humans to help you out. You know, because you aren't perfect."

The corner of his mouth pulls up as he watches me. "You really are something, aren't you?"

I shrug. "Don't look much into it."

"Rahym!"

We both twist our heads to see Fatma standing at the entrance to the Door Stop. An exuberant smile plays across her face as she looks at me.

"It's Jennet." Despite her smile, icy fear clenches my gut at what that could mean. "She's awake."

CHAPTER 23

J ennet can't seem to keep her fingers still as she takes in the news. They keep tapping against each other or threading together or splaying apart or cracking the individual knuckles. She looks pale and weak as she sits up on her pallet. Her eyes are unfocused as she stares into the fire.

"Sena is...dead?" she whispers.

When I first came in from my conversation with Nakir, I thought she might have lost her mind, too, because she's been so silent. So to hear her speak, even with the bad news, makes that tight muscle deep inside my chest loosen. Just a tiny bit.

Fatma can't seem to stop looking at Jennet, like she's some sort of specter from beyond the grave. And, really, she truly is. There's something about her that seems to be transparent, like she's so fragile, she can just be shattered easily.

Kerem stays at Jennet's side, a shadow to her light.

Jennet is the one who keeps the witches grounded. She's the one that makes them more whole.

Nakir nods solemnly in answer to her question, and her hands cover her mouth, trembling against her skin. Tears fall down her cheeks in rivulets, and she's not really seeing anyone but her own pain.

"Oh my god," Jennet whispers, her voice shaky, breathless. "I—I was the one who—"

"It's not your fault," Fatma says, reaching out across the space between them. Jennet's eyes flick to the younger witch, horror in her gaze.

Then her face crumples, and she leans forward on herself. "If only I could have been a little stronger!" she cries, rocking herself. "If only..."

If only, if only, if only...

Our lives in the shadow of the curse are filled with "if onlys." When you only have so much energy, you start to question everything you do with that energy. If you had done enough. Jennet doesn't think she did enough.

And it breaks my heart to see that look on her face.

"I should have known that I could have transferred energy," Jennet sobs. "I should have—"

"You didn't know," Fatma says gently. "You are the only witch to possess power like yours. You couldn't have known."

"I didn't push myself then. I didn't—"

"Jennet," Kerem finally speaks, an edge to his voice. "*Stop.*"

To everyone's surprise, she does, keeping her hand clamped over her mouth, her eyes wide.

"You saved us," Nakir says softly. "I know you keep blaming yourself for it—believe me, I've been there myself." I wonder if he's speaking about his time with the old group of Halos. He's been on this earth for a long time. I'm sure he has a ton of regrets that have put him in Jennet's position.

"But if you and Sena hadn't put yourself out there in harm's way," Nakir says, giving Jennet's fingers a squeeze—fingers that I've tried willing back to life so many times over

ERIN HAYES & REBECCA HAMILTON

the past few days, "none of us would be here right now. We'd all be dead, and our only hope for lifting the curse would be gone."

"But—"

"We knew this was a distinct possibility," Emre says, speaking up for the first time in a while. His throat is raspy as well. Jennet looks at him. "We all went into this knowing that there was a big chance that we weren't going to make it out."

Jennet passes a hand through her hair. "Yes," she says. "But—"

"We can't give up now," Kerem says. "We've gone too far. And if we stop, then we're sullying Sena's memory."

Finally, that seems to break through to Jennet. I can see the change in her face as she reflects on those words. Her eyes cut over toward me, giving me a questioning glance that I am not sure I understand.

She clears her throat and looks back at Nakir. "Can I see her?"

The angel nods. "We buried her outside."

Jennet blanches at that, and I wonder what funeral plans Sena did have in her life. Did she have family back home that was waiting for her to wake up, to give them a better future?

Jennet gets to her feet, her knees visibly wobbly as she stands. Fatma reaches out to help her. "No," Jennet says, waving her off. "I've got this. I'm all right."

I know from her voice that she isn't all right. But she doesn't even glance in my direction again as she leaves the Door Stop. No one else leaves to go to her.

———

"I WANTED TO BE ALONE, RAHYM."

Jennet doesn't even turn around as she stands in front of

the fresh mound of dirt that signifies where we put Sena to rest. There are no markers for the grave, as demonlings would use it to dig her up for lunch, but I wonder what Jennet thinks of it. If we didn't do right by Sena's memory.

"I know," I tell her. "But from experience, I know you shouldn't be alone too long."

Jennet sighs, crossing her arms over her chest. "We've all been alone too long. Sena was my teacher. When I first joined the witches. Fatma and Kerem were her students, too, but Sena was more like a mother to me. She took care of me when no one else wanted anything to do with an orphaned witch, and...I failed her."

Even from behind, she looks tired, worn out like a pair of trousers that should have been thrown out years ago. And there's a sadness to her that I'm afraid I won't be able to reach.

I put a hand on her shoulder and give what I hope is a comforting squeeze. Her body is stiff beneath my touch, unyielding.

"Hey," I whisper. "It's not your fault. You can't blame—"

Jennet whirls on me, her blue eyes flashing in anger. "It is my fault!" she cries. Her voice is wavering, uneven. "If I could have held on for just a little longer, I could have...I could have..."

She's beautiful.

Her anger is a welcome departure from grief. Anger is the fire in the Door to Hell. Anger keeps you alive when you've lost everything dear to you.

Look at you being sentimental.

Sentimental. Right. And I'm not being sentimental enough.

Before I can think too much about it—because, let's face it, when you have two minds at odds with each other, you

171

tend to think a lot—I wrap her up in an embrace. At first, she stands stiff against me before she sighs brokenly and leans into me. It's a sign of trust, not weakness, that she's doing this.

Hope she knows it too.

I don't give her platitudes. I don't tell her that everything is going to be all right or that we'll succeed where Sena couldn't. I don't want to lie to her, because while I've been a bad man in my time, I don't want there to be any lies between us.

Jennet relaxes into me, her shoulders heaving with the silent sobs that wrack her body. I hold her, putting my chin on top of her head, trying to bring her back to us.

To me.

"You were right," she whispers into my shoulder. "You were right about everything."

No. Not everything. Not by a long shot.

I've been wrong about so many things in my life. So many mistakes.

"You said that this was going to be a suicide mission," Jennet continues. "You told me that we'd die on this. And…I stupidly thought that there was no way that we'd die. Because we were doing what was right and that we *couldn't* die. And…"

"Hey." I pull her back to look down at her. "You came at a time when I thought there was nothing left worth saving. And you changed that for me, Jennet. You taught me that there was so much more to fight for."

She shakes her head. "Is there? When everything is so fucked?"

"Yes."

My lips crash against hers, continuing where we left off

the other night. I wasn't ready then, because I didn't know how much I had left to lose, but now, I refuse to lose her.

At first, she doesn't respond to my kiss, and I cup her cheek along her jaw, coaxing her mouth to open with my tongue. When she does part her lips, I explore every inch of her that I can. I cherish every sensation, every moment spent with her where she fills up my senses, and I never want to let that go.

I've kissed her in the past, but this *feels* different to me. Different than anything I've ever felt in my life. There's a fieriness to her that burns brighter than the desert, where burning along with her is the best thing ever for a starving man.

"Rahym," she breathes into my skin, her need so evident. Hell, I'm sure that she can feel my own need pressed up against her. "Rahym, I—"

I kiss her again before she can say anything that breaks the magic of this moment. All I want is her and to feel alive again and for her to feel alive, too. This time, she does kiss me back, grabbing onto the back of my neck as she holds onto this wild ride that we're both on.

I don't ever want it to stop.

"I want you," I whisper to her. "I need you, *Jennet*."

Her eyes flutter open as she stares at me. I'm begging her for permission with my eyes, but I realize that she's begging me, too. Begging me to let her into my own life, to move on from the past and face a better future, together.

"I've been waiting for you to say that for so long," she tells me. "*So long*."

I lose all willpower to stop. I crush her against me, losing myself in her. How could someone as strong as her be so small in my arms? When my whole world is filled up with just *her*.

I backpedal, taking her with me to the other side of the Door Stop. Away from the view of Sena's grave and far away from the other Halos so they don't find us. In the eastern side of the cave system, there's a shady little alcove that's sheltered from the elements.

Not the most romantic of places, but neither of us cares at the moment. We just care about being together.

She tugs off my tattered shirt, still burned from the firestorm. Kerem fully healed me a few days ago, but her fingertips trace where my skin is scarred and shinier from the burns. Scars that I'll likely carry for the rest of my life.

Her eyebrows pinch together, and I can see the guilt in her eyes. She's blaming herself again. So I kiss her to take her mind far away. When my fingers slip past the waistband of her pants to feel her wet slickness, she bucks against me with a gasp, her eyes opening wide.

You're taking her far *away from there.*

My need becomes too great as I work to take off her shirt. I have to see her. Know that she's *mine*. She groans in disappointment as my fingers leave her to frantically pull up her tunic, but when our gazes meet again, she stills, shivering.

Then I take in the sight of her.

Her skin is flawless. She had been completely healed after everything, and there's nothing marring her expanse of smooth, bronzed skin.

"You're beautiful," I whisper. "And I love every beautiful inch of you."

Her bottom lip trembles. "You love—?"

I kiss her again before she can finish her question. Call me a coward—whether it's out of embarrassment or because I'm afraid she doesn't feel the same way, I don't want to stop this moment right now.

I just want *her.*

She groans against me as I knead one of her breasts. We make our way to the ground, and she straddles me as my hands roam down her body, worshipping every inch of her. I cup her ass to me as she leans forward, kissing me, her hand rubbing the stubble on my face as the other trails down my chest, under my own trousers, and...

My breath catches as her fingers wrap around my hard length. I can feel her smiling against me at my reaction, and she gives me a firm stroke.

I almost lose myself then.

Cradling her against me, I roll her onto her back with me on top of her. She looks up at me with wonder and amazement in her eyes, just as I'm sure it's reflected in mine, that we're here. Together.

She kisses me again, more frantic, more fervent as she tugs off my trousers, and I do the same to her. There's too much clothing barring us from each other, and it isn't until she's completely exposed to me, skin to skin, that I realize that my heart is about to beat out of my chest.

That fluttering feeling I've had ever since reconnected with her? I know what it is now. And I haven't felt anything like it in so damn long.

"I love you, too," she whispers finally. As if reading my thoughts.

I can't take it anymore. I hold myself above her, afraid to crush her, but there's so much trust in her eyes, that I—

She arches backward, a rough cry careening through her body as I enter her slowly, enough to get the feel of her body around me, stretching to let me fit. Her breasts heave, glistening in sweat, and I lick it from her, trying to do anything to hold on as long as I can.

"Okay," she says hoarsely. She positions herself beneath me, to get the angle just right. "Okay, I'm ready."

I start to move then, trying to be gentle, although it's so damn hard with her beautiful body beneath mine. Her fingernails dig into my back, and she holds on for dear life as I thrust myself into her.

This is worth fighting for.

Jennet is worth fighting for.

She comes, rocking her hips against me. She throws her head back with a strangled cry, my name echoing off the granite around us. I bend over to possess her mouth, and as I come myself, it's her name that I say into her lips, into her mouth, into her soul.

I pull myself back to get a good look at her. Whether it's from the heat or if it's from embarrassment, her cheeks are flushed as she gazes up at me, something akin to wonder in her eyes as she traces a finger along my cheek.

I thought I'd never be this happy again.

"*Rahym,*" she whispers, like my name is the most beautiful thing on her lips.

I pull myself out of her, and I pull her to me as we both lay together, our limbs and sweat and breaths tangled up together.

Neither of us says anything more. Because for now, I just want to rest. To be with Jennet.

My new to-do list should have one thing at the very top:

1. *Love Jennet*

THE FUNNY THING IS, I don't think I'll need a reminder. Not for the rest of my life.

CHAPTER 24

"I've never tried it before," Jennet says as she's curled up against me. "But I've always wanted to see if it worked. Extending the, ah, pleasure with my power."

She's being coy and shy, despite the fact that we've been laying in the alcove next to the Door Stop all day, making love when words didn't say enough. So much history between us. So many times when I should have said something and didn't.

And now...we're together.

I know that we're using plenty of energy having sex, but I don't want it to stop. Common sense dictates that we shouldn't be expending everything on this, but we aren't going anywhere today, and I just want to spend as much time as possible reminding ourselves why we're fighting.

I chuckle and kiss her forehead. "So you're saying it wasn't me that gave you the best sex of your life?"

She raises an eyebrow, peering up at me. God, she looks beautiful when she's playful like this. Like she doesn't have the weight of the world on her shoulders. "Oh, trust me, that was all *you*. I just gave you a boost to make better for both of us."

"So you're saying I shouldn't be disappointed in myself?"

She snorts. "No, you *definitely* shouldn't be disappointed." She pauses, mulling over her next question, and I close my eyes, waiting for it. I could guess what it is going to be, and I'm still trying to figure it out myself, but…

"Are you okay?" she asks softly. "With this?"

"Why wouldn't I be?" I murmur softly.

"It's just…Maysa and your daughter…I don't want you thinking that I'm trying to replace them."

I draw circles on her back with my fingers, feeling the smooth expanse of her skin against mine. I could spend the rest of my life exploring her.

"I think I'm on the way to being all right," I say honestly. "I don't think of this as moving on, but…*living*. And I think Maysa would have wanted that."

"I wish I could have seen you two together. With your daughter."

"Beste would have liked you," I say, knowing full well that it's true. "She always liked being around strong role models."

Jennet curls up against me, holding me tightly, like she doesn't want to let go. "I've wanted this for years."

"I could just lay here forever," I murmur, laying back.

"Me, too." Despite this, she moves away from me, and I let out a groan. "But we should go back in. It's almost sundown, and I do believe you've nearly worn me out."

A smile plays across my lips as I watch her get dressed. She's right—we don't want to be out here after dark, and I can feel myself slipping as the hours have gone by.

"I'm surprised the others haven't come out to check up on us," she says.

"I'm not." I know Nakir, and I know that he would know better than to come out here looking for us. I'm sure he can guess exactly what happened the second I followed Jennet out here.

Clever bastard.

I get my clothes on, taking some of my time and energy to kiss Jennet, stroke her hair, do everything I can to make this magic last as long as possible.

Jennet slows as we pass by Sena's grave. Her hands leave mine as she kneels in front of the mound, pressing her fingertips to her lips in good-bye. She stays silently like this for several minutes. I don't rush her. I don't try to pressure her either way. I let her do what she needs to do for how long she needs to do it.

The shadows lengthen around us as she sits. Finally, she gets to her feet, her eyes glistening, and she gives me a small smile.

"Okay," she whispers, taking my hand again. "Let's get going."

We make our way back to the entrance to the Door Stop, where Murat is sitting toward the entrance, guarding it. He raises an eyebrow as we pass him.

"Where have you two been?" he asks. There's no jealousy in his voice, so I just smile serenely at him.

"Just out and about."

He scoffs, looking between Jennet and me. "Don't tell me Emre and Rabia were with you guys."

Jennet blushes and keeps walking farther into the Door Stop to join Fatma and Kerem. Both of the witches wrap her up in a hug, relief evident on their face. Nakir gives me an appraising nod as he passes by.

"Where did Emre and Rabia go?" I ask.

"Out," Nakir says.

"We ran out of fresh water," Murat adds. "They went to go see if they could find some nearby."

Of course. Because our stop here has been far longer than we anticipated. "Do they know know how to find water out here?" I put my hands in my pockets, looking back out the entrance to the Door Stop.

A grin ghosts on Nakir's features. "Well, that's the big question, isn't it? He's ex-Army from *before*, so I think if anyone can find water, it would be him. Plus, Rabia is, well, Rabia." He frowns, and I get what he means. Rabia is part feral in her own right, and I imagine out of all of us, she'd be the best one to sniff out water. "We're not critical at the moment, but it would be good if we found some."

"Yeah," I agree softly, looking around the Door Stop. Everyone else has settled into their routine. "So I guess we continue tomorrow morning?"

Nakir nods. "We have a long way to go still. How was it out there?" He can't help his sly grin, so I match it.

"Fine. Jennet and I talked."

"Right. Talked." He claps me on the back. "Glad you two found some common ground after everything you've been through. You deserve it."

Murat looks up at me with a confused expression. "You two talked for that long?"

"Uh, yeah," I say, not wanting to get into my sex life with him of all people.

"Oh." The man frowns. "Here I thought you were having wild sex out there."

I burst out laughing. Murat gives me another bewildered look as I join Jennet and the others, not wanting to be apart from her too long. There's something different about the way she looks at me now, as I'm sure is the other way around too. I look at her like she's the most precious thing in world.

She is.

I think back to what she said earlier, about if I'm all right with moving on. I truly don't think of it as moving on but more…trying to find my way in world that's less than perfect. I'm not sullying their memory, but I'm hoping to do right by them in having a purpose to my life now.

I suddenly see Jennet's optimism and her hope with everything. It doesn't seem impossible anymore. Not when there's wonderful things in this world. Not when I have her.

I close my eyes. *Thank you, Maysa.*

Thank you, Jennet.

Just as I sit down next to Jennet, there's a scream at the entrance to the Door. It's not demonlings.

It's Murat.

His scream is suddenly cut short, followed by a painful gurgle. The horses whinny in fear at the noise, possibly smelling something on the air that I can't.

I spring to my feet and look for my yataghan among my belongings on the floor. It takes entirely too long to find my weapon, but I pull it up and out of the sheath as I round out toward the front of the cave.

"What's happening?" Fatma cries, getting to her feet. "What's—"

I shush her, trying to put myself between the entrance and the three witches. I exchange a glance with Nakir as we head to the front of the cave. He draws out his sword, wielding it in front of us.

He gives a knowing nod as he steps out in front of me. I look at Jan, the sword gleaming in the dying light as Nakir pads ahead. Kerem rushes by me, obviously intent on healing Murat.

If it's not too late. That just puts him closer to danger.

"Jennet," I say, turning around. "Stay back with Fatma."

She gives a nod, her eyes fierce as she puts herself in front of Fatma.

I'd been fearless before when I thought I had nothing to live for. But now, as I follow Nakir to the front of the cave, I'm terrified. I don't want anything to happen to Jennet. Not now, not when we've just found each other.

Nury grabs his own weapon, a scimitar, and falls into step beside me. He looks terrified as well, but I recognize his expression. He'd do anything to protect Fatma.

Here's hoping that we are up against something that we can defeat.

Kerem is sitting in front of Murat, who had been run through with a spear, effectively pinning him to the wall. That must have been the first scream. Then someone—or something—slashed his throat all the way to his spine, killing him. Blood spurts from the wound.

There's nothing to be done. Kerem can't heal him if he's dead.

The male witch sits back with a curse under his breath and rubs his hands on his face.

"The weapons look like they're from demonlings," Nury says, glancing to me. "But…"

"It's not just demonlings," Nakir says from the entrance. His voice is low, dangerous. He sounds pissed. I follow him to the lip of the Door Stop and look down at the horde below us.

Firelight highlights the edges of the army. There are fewer demonlings here than the horde that attacked us, but these are bigger, meaner, more battle-hardened. It's like the Door to Hell held back this group for when we were most tired.

How the hell did they sneak up on Murat when he was keeping watch and where Fatma couldn't sense them? Magic?

Or is something else masking them?

I may see why. At the front of the pack is the biggest demonling I've ever seen. He's even bigger than Nakir, his red skin almost scarlet. His black hair is tied back, and his eyes are as black as coal, including his irises.

But the thing most disconcerting about him are his wings. Demonlings don't have wings, at least not any demonlings that I've seen. So why is he different? The wingspan is about twelve feet, with sinewy, leather skin wrapped along thin bones. I'm not sure if the wings are able to hold him aloft, but they're imposing enough.

I get a feel for what Nakir would have looked like as a fully-fledged angel before he fell from heaven.

The huge demonling's eyes are locked on Nakir as the two of them have a staring match amongst themselves. Finally, he takes a burlap sack from the demonling next to him and tosses it our way. The sack hits the sand and bounces once before whatever is inside it rolls out.

I feel like I'm going to be sick. In a bloody heap, Rabia's head rolls out and faces us, her mouth open in a permanent scream.

She had been decapitated during her travels with Emre. And just as I wonder what happened to Emre, the old, wizened soldier steps out from the huge demonling's shadow and crosses his arms as he looks up at Nakir.

"What the hell is happening?" Nury whispers beside me.

Nakir clears his throat. "I didn't expect to see you here yet," he says, "*Abaddon.*"

Suddenly, I know why the demonling in front of us is so huge. Because he's not a demonling at all.

This is Abaddon. The Demon Lord who has cursed us for

the past fifty years. The entire purpose of our journey. So close, and yet so impossible right now. We're far outnumbered by manpower and by numbers.

There's no way we'll win.

Abaddon grins up at Nakir. "Hello, brother. Aren't you happy to see me?"

CHAPTER 25

I stare down at Emre, unable to process what the fuck he's doing standing next to the Demon Lord like he is. Bile twists in my stomach, threatening to upheave as it hits me.

"You betrayed us," I say blandly. "You sold us out to the Demon Lord."

There's apology floating in the old man's eyes, even as he looks up at us. It takes me a moment to understand *that*. That he'd feel remorse after what he did. "I did what I had to do," he says.

"You *had* to betray us?" Nury exclaims.

Kerem comes to our side. Three men, plus three witches, against Abaddon himself. I don't like our odds, but I'll be damned if I'm going to let him anywhere near Jennet. Not while I'm still alive.

"What was the deal?" I say through gritted teeth. "When did you make it?"

Emre lifts a shoulder. "The deal was if I help Abaddon dispose of the Halos then he would grant my family a pass at the curse. Release them from it."

"I thought you didn't have family," Nury says dumbly.

"Oh yes," Emre says. "An ailing wife, and my kids and grandkids are stuck in this...*thing*...this curse. There's no way we could have succeeded."

"No," Nakir says. "There was no way, especially with you sabotaging us."

I blink, feeling my entire body go cold. "When the Lodge burned down," I whisper. "That was you?"

Emre averts his eyes. "Nothing against you, Rahym," he says softly. "I really liked you. I just did what I had to do."

I clench my fist. "It has *everything* to do with me," I growl. These assholes are the reason I lost everything. From the fires and the demonling attack to the wildfire storm—how much of that was Emre being in contact with Abaddon? How many times did he betray our position or our state in order to get on the Demon Lord's good side?

"Tell me," Nakir says, his voice low and dangerous, "were you the one to kill Rabia, or was that one of these other fuckers out here?"

Even from this distance, I can see Emre swallow uncomfortably. That's all the answer that Nakir needs. He swings the sword toward the soldier, the blade cutting through the air. Simultaneously, Abaddon holds up a hand. The attack gets blocked by an invisible barrier that only sparks and hisses at the strikes, effectively protecting the demon and the horde.

All of them except for Emre. I see as the arc slices through the man at the neck. He blinks confusedly for a moment, his mouth working painfully. Then blood spills from a cut on his neck as his head slides off it and onto the ground. The rest of Emre collapses afterward.

Decapitated. A fitting way to kill the man who betrayed us and cut off Rabia's head. Nakir believes in second chances up to a point, but this took it too far for him. I can see his fury boiling just below the surface.

I don't feel any sadness for Emre. Too much energy wasted.

"So glad you were able to take care of that," Abaddon says, his low, powerful voice rumbling throughout the landscape. "Good help is so hard to find these days. Especially when anyone can betray you at the drop of a hat."

"Well, he saved us the rest of a long, hard trip," Nakir shoots back. "Because, well, he brought you to us." And he grins at the Demon Lord, his smile too sugary sweet for it to be natural.

Abaddon reflects the grin in his own face, only this one is more sinister. Demon and angel, squaring off against each other. "Well, I'm here now." He spreads his arms open wide. "What do you want?"

Nakir raises his blade. "Your death!"

It is the first time I've ever really seen Nakir lose his cool. He looks like a demon himself, baring his teeth.

He rushes forward, and Abaddon smiles almost serenely as he draws his kilij from its scabbard. "I was hoping you'd say that."

A loud clang rings through the night as the two swords meet. Even though Nakir's sword is huge compared to Abaddon's kilij, the demon's weapon holds up to force of the bigger blade. The two tussle, dodging parries and attacks.

It's a fight between two extremes. Nakir against the bigger Abaddon. Abaddon's kilij against Jan. They move at such speeds that I can barely keep up. Nakir swings the blade up, but Abaddon catches it, beckoning Nakir forward, teasing him as he coaxes the angel forward, deeper into the throng of demonlings.

I look down at them, blinking as I had been so distracted. The horde sneers up at us as one, daring us to fight them.

Waiting.

For what?

Jennet's still within the Door, her power nearly dwindled. As is mine. As is all of ours. Including Nakir.

How much has he done today? I was so preoccupied with Jennet all day, I don't know what state anyone else is in or how much energy they have left. We're facing off against these demonlings, and Nakir is unable to use the same attacks he did the other night when he hacked through hundreds of demonlings at once.

Without that, we're sitting ducks.

He's using up everything he has against this demon. The rage is blinding him to it, and I don't know if there's any way I can pull him out of it.

Maybe, if I can just get to Nakir...

Go.

I don't need to be told twice.

I run down the hill, noting how much slower I'm moving compared to the angel when he crossed the same distance.

"Rahym!" Nury yells behind me. "*Rahym!*"

I don't hear him as my yataghan clashes with the kilij. Abaddon blinks at me, as if in surprise that I'm down here. Hell, I'm surprised myself, but I roar and rear back, swinging my sword in a downward arc as I meet Nakir's eyes, telling him in my gaze when I want him to do. I'm not the greatest swordsman, not by a long shot, but I can make a difference in a fight like this.

I see the angel smirk, completely in tune with me.

That's right, Nakir.

I just need to distract Abaddon long enough for Nakir to make the final killing blow. Now we're on one side, battling against the torrent of strikes from Abaddon. And for one crazy moment, I think we are pushing him back, away from Jennet and the rest of the Halos.

This is what I've been working toward for most of my life. This is the end of the journey. And if I can just hold out long enough…

I hear more clangs as Nury and Kerem join me, roaring their own battle cries as they clash with the demonlings. Outnumbered, so damn outnumbered, but so close in this final moment. We can do this.

We just have to hold out.

I hear a clang unlike any other before it, and I stupidly flinch while trying to figure it out.

What the fuck was that?

I have no idea. What the hell.

Crazily—*stupidly, dumbly*—I watch as Nakir's sword, Jan flies through the air, yards from our battle. There's a hand attached to it, still holding on.

Nakir's hand.

I glance back at the angel, who stands stiffly, but there's nothing holding up his limbs anymore.

He's empty.

I haven't seen the angel lose his energy like this ever. Usually he's so reserved, so in control. And now, seeing it happen at the worst time possible, a hysterical feeling over-comes me at the absurdity that something horrible like *this* would happen *now.*

Not now. Not now!

Nakir meets my eyes, and I see the light leave them as he topples to the side.

Okay, yes. This is happening now.

Angel down.

Without thinking about the consequences of it, because

the alternative is that much worse, I drop my yataghan, spurring my muscles to move for the angel sword. There's surprisingly no one to intercept me on my way—maybe they're being distracted by everything else, including an angel falling before their very eyes.

I make it to the sword, reach for the handle, pull, and…

It doesn't budge.

I blink once as a different kind of panic sets in.

Fuck. No, no, no, no.

I try to lift it again. The sword, so big and heavy, is immovable. Which is impossible, because Nakir carried it on his back wherever we were. I always thought it was heavy, but Nakir never had trouble, so I figured there has been something to make it lighter than it seemed. After all, he wielded it like it was a steak knife.

And now that I'm trying to lift it, the damn thing won't move at all.

No, please lift. Please lift. Please lift!

I get to about an inch off the ground before everything fails me, my energy leaves me. As I fight to stay awake, I see Abaddon in my line of sight, chuckling darkly as he hefts Jan, like it weighs as little as Nakir always made it seem. He holds it in one hand, examining the length of it, trying out the weight of it.

He makes it look easy.

"Poor human," he croons. "What interesting creatures you are. You're willing to sacrifice so much to make your lives easier. Don't you know that I'm a prisoner on this plane as much as you?"

Even though I can't move, I watch in horror as he stalks over to Nakir with the sword.

This can't be happening. This just can't—

He drives the sword right through the angel's chest. The

angel, having his energy depleted, doesn't even make a sound as I hear the sword break through his rib cage, straight to his heart.

No.

I hear someone screaming or sobbing. It sounds like Jennet. She can't be out here. They can't see her. Not like this.

It's not Nakir's name that she calls. It's mine.

"Rahym!"

Abaddon stands over me, something akin to pity on his face. Then, wordlessly, he lifts a blade—his kilij, I realize, the angel sword still stuck through Nakir's chest—and drives it right through my own chest.

CHAPTER 26

"This can't be the end for you. You know that, right?"

The voice is familiar, so close to me that I can reach out and touch it. It reverberates throughout my soul, bringing me back to some of the best times in my life.

"Maysa," I whisper, reaching out toward her.

Her face appears within my hands, beaming at me, although there's something akin to sadness there.

"My love," she whispers, turning her cheek into the palm of my hand so she can kiss it.

Guilt ricochets through me as I watch her, so unexpected. I hiss in a sharp breath. When I'm with Jennet, the world feels right. But when I remember Maysa too much, I...

Our eyes meet.

"Don't." Maysa says the word so softly, I flinch. "Don't you dare feel guilty about living your life, Rahym."

"I—"

"Trust me." A smile pulls at her full lips. "Both Beste and I want you to be happy."

I open my mouth to say something to her, but there's a

familiar giggle, and I turn, almost in shock at the young girl who flings herself into my arms.

"Daddy!" Beste cries, and I stand, holding her, shocked.

My throat closes up, and I wonder how I ever lived for three years without Beste to hold onto. To have her call me Daddy or to have me check under the bed for demonlings. My baby girl is in my arms, and I don't ever want to let her go. Her hair feels so real against my palm, softer than my hair and the same color as Maysa's.

How can you ever say good-bye to her, Rahym?

How indeed. Beste's scent fills up my senses, a mix of figs and honey soap. I close my eyes and inhale it deeply. How did I ever forget even a tiny bit of what she smells like?

Maysa chuckles and puts her hands on her hips as she regards us with an amused smile. "As you can see, we're both doing fine, Rahym."

Still clutching Beste to me, I look at my dead wife. "I—"

She cups my cheek and smiles at me. "You have to keep living in the present, my love. Not in the past. Beste and I will be waiting for you. But you can't give up now. You can't let the world down."

"I don't know how I'm supposed to help," I whisper to her.

She sighs. "You'll find a way. I always knew you were special. And that you'd do big things. It's not your time. You're not supposed to be here yet."

"I don't want to leave you."

"I know. But we are doing all right."

"There's no more bedtime for me," Beste says, beaming up at me.

I don't know if that's supposed to make me feel better, but I hiccup a laugh. "Your momma's been breaking the rules," I tell her.

Beste only responds with a roll of her eyes. I actually chuckle at that. Even at her age, she reminds me way too much of her mother. *"Daddy."*

"What Beste means to say," Maysa says with a laugh, pulling our daughter back into her arms, "is that there is no rush. We'll be right here waiting for you *when* it's your time. Not before."

"And if I fall in love with someone else?" I manage

"You mean Jennet?" Maysa laughs. "There's no one else I would have wanted it to happen with. She was your first love."

"You were my first life."

Her face softens. "And nothing is going to change that," she says. "But the world is a wide, wide place. Full of happiness and sorrow. And there's plenty of room for you to live your life as you need."

She gives me a chaste kiss on my lips. "Now, *go.*"

TEARS DRIP on my cheeks like raindrops, and for a crazed moment, I wonder if I've woken up in a part of the world where rain falls from the sky. It rains in Turkmenistan but so rarely and sparsely, the earth drinks it up the instant it falls.

Maybe I'm far away from the pain of being stabbed through with a sword.

Jennet's face swims above mine, her eyes red-rimmed. Like she's been crying.

"Oh my god," she exclaims, holding my head in her lap. *"Rahym!* You're alive!"

I grimace, but my body aches so much, I don't even bother trying to sit up. I know it will hurt too much. Instead, I just blink up at her, assessing my injuries as they come to me.

My chest aches where Abaddon drove a sword through it. Holy shit, I was *dead.* I had the Demon Lord run me through. Just like Nakir. His body flashes in my mind, the sword hacked through his chest.

"What happened?" I croak.

A mix of emotions washes over Jennet's face. She's afraid to tell me everything at once, which means that it must be bad. Which means that she's worried about exacerbating whatever's left of my wounds.

"Abaddon…nearly killed you," Jennet whispers, starting from the top. The easiest one.

"How *didn't* he?"

"It's because you're a lucky son of a bitch," Kerem scoffs under his breath. I hadn't even noticed that he was nearby. I twist my head to look at him curiously. He rubs at his face. "I had only had just enough energy for you *not* to die."

That explains why I feel like I've been run over by a wagon. Or a horde of demonlings, which is probably the case.

"What happened?" I demand. "Where's Nakir?"

Jennet and Kerem exchange wary glances. "They took him. They took the sword and him," Jennet says softly. "Probably to the Watchtower."

Fuck. The angel and the angel sword. Gone.

I try to look around to see what else is happening. "Where's Nury? And Fatma?"

At those two names, I hear a sob to my left, and I see Fatma sitting by herself, her arms wrapped around her legs. She's alive, but based on her expression…

"Nury's dead," she sobs, angrily pawing at her eyes. "He's dead and I…and I…" She cries even harder, her entire body shaking in the moonlight. "I lost him. I lost Nury!"

Kerem scoots over to her and wraps her up in a hug. "I'm so sorry," he whispers to her. "I'm so goddamn sorry."

She cries into his shoulder, inconsolable in her grief. "If only I had been able to sense the demonlings. I could have…I could have…"

"I told you," Kerem tells her softly, "Abaddon must have been masking them somehow. Keeping them from us. There's no way we could have done anything different."

I hope it's some bad dream, that this isn't real. That maybe what I saw with Maysa and Beste is the real world and this is a nightmare that I'll wake up from.

Surely he's alive now.

Jennet's face is fearsome as she watches Kerem console Fatma. "His injuries were too extensive for Kerem," she murmurs softly. "He had been…badly hurt."

Even more so than being stabbed through the chest. I know better than to ask for more clarification. Not with Fatma so close by.

Jennet wets her lips, and I feel her arms tighten around me protectively. I wonder if she's thinking about me being killed like Nury.

"Why did they leave us?" I muse. "Abaddon had us. Why didn't he just kill us?"

Jennet stills, considering her answer. "It's arrogance. He got everything he needed when he killed Nakir," she whispers. "He got the sword. He killed the only person who could stop him. He's won."

I place my hand over hers and give it a squeeze. "No." I grit my teeth. "No, he hasn't."

I groan as I force myself to sit up. I wave away Jennet's hands as she tries to help me—friends of ours just died; I can sit up my own damn self. It takes a lot out of me, and I huff with pained breaths.

"Rahym—" Jennet starts.

I wince as I get to my feet. "We need to head to the Watchtower."

Jennet's expression goes from surprised to incredulous as she looks up at me. "What? *Now?*"

Fatma and Kerem both watch us, too, like they don't understand what we're saying.

I close my eyes and stagger under the wave of pain that wipes over me. I comb a hand through my hair, tugging at it so it stands straight up. My chest burns, feeling like it will pull apart if I move too much. However Kerem knitted me back together, it feels like only a temporary thing. I rub at it, just to make sure that I'm still in one piece.

"Abaddon won't expect us to be coming after him so quickly," I reason. "If we leave now, we have a better shot at catching him by surprise."

Jennet frowns. "But the Watchtower…"

"He made it over there."

"He *flew*."

"And we have Akhal-Teke horses," I say, gesturing to the Door Stop where I hope our horses are still alive. No one contradicts me, so I take that as confirmation that I'm correct. "They're legendary for their speed. We've been conserving our energy during our journey because we've always had supplies, and we've been careful not to overextend it."

"And you want us to overextend it?" Kerem asks tiredly.

I gesture helplessly. "If we catch him by surprise—"

"There *is no surprise!*" Fatma shouts, her anger coloring her cheeks. "You're going up against a Demon Lord! He's more powerful and smarter than any of us! And he will kill us!"

I look to Jennet. "That's why we do something incredibly stupid, then."

Even my comment is stupid, but the corner of her mouth quirks up as she reaches out and takes my hand. My crazy lover, ready to fight with me to the ends of the earth.

We have to do this. There's no other choice.

"Okay." She nods. *"Okay."*

CHAPTER 27

A lion looks none too impressed as I saddle him up for the journey. A few days of relaxation has made him more belligerent than ever, but I'm glad the bastard is still alive.

"Yeah, you're still stuck with me. Sorry."

He flicks his ear in irritation.

The demonlings didn't kill any of the horses, much to my relief.

We have seven horses among the four of us. I know that we'll be pushing the horses we're riding harder than those that don't have riders, so we can alternate for fresher horses if ours slow down.

How far away is the Watchtower? How much more strength do we have after this?

I glance back at Jennet, Kerem, and Fatma. Jennet is the only one with any light in her eyes. Fatma remains silent, her expression understandably in a scowl, her eyes red with tears that keep falling over her cheeks. I clear my throat, wondering if there's anything I can say to her to ease her

ERIN HAYES & REBECCA HAMILTON

pain. I feel like a complete ass because we don't have the time
nor the spare energy to bury Nury's body. I marked the Door
Stop's spot on the map. When we come back through here
—*if* we survive—I'll give Nury a proper burial.

Nury and Rabia both. Two Halos who deserve the best
for everything they've worked towards.

I make that silent promise to myself. I don't say it to
Fatma, as I'm sure she hates me. And pretty much all of life
at the moment. My heart aches for her. I've been in her situation before. I know what it's like to lose those you love.

Kerem seems shell-shocked as well, but he just clenches
his jaw and moves with the mechanical efficiency of a man
who isn't sure where his life is going. Again, another trait I
recognize in myself. I don't have time to give him any encouraging words. I tried thanking him, but the man brushed it off.

He saved me when he couldn't save Nury. I can't imagine
how much that must weigh on him.

"We ride at full-speed to the Watchtower," I tell Jennet as
she swings herself up into her saddle. "I'll lead."

Jennet nods, making sure that her second horse is tethered
correctly to her saddle. "All right." Her skin is pallid, her
anxieties playing across her face.

I give her thigh a squeeze. "Hey," I tell her, "I won't let
anything happen to you."

She looks stricken for a moment. "That's what I'm afraid
of," she whispers.

Her horse paws impatiently at the ground. Unlike Alion,
her mount is ready and anxious to get a move on.

Makes me wonder if Alion is a purebred Akhal-Teke,
because I have to coax him away from the wall. He'd rather
just eat feed than go out into the darkness.

I guess I'm the same way, too, I muse as I swing a leg up
into Alion's saddle. He huffs angrily and sidesteps until I get

him under control. I give his hindquarter a playful slap, and he swishes his tail angrily.

Some things never change.

"Are you two ready?" I ask, looking over to Kerem and Fatma, who have already mounted their horses. Everyone except Fatma has a spare horse tethered to their saddles, for a grand total of seven horses. Seven horses who were bred for speed.

We can make it.

The animals look ready to run and gallop, but the two witches look like they're barely holding themselves together.

"Yes," Kerem says softly.

I clack the reins as I drive Alion to the edge of the Door Stop. I pass by our tent rolls, our camp gear, our rugs.

We're traveling as light as possible, which may be a suicide mission, but at this point, we're too far to head back and too far not to keep going for the Watchtower. All nonessentials are left behind.

If we succeed, we can pick them up on our way back.

If we fail, well, then it won't matter anyway.

Maybe the next group of Halos will find it and it will help them in their quest.

I almost laugh out loud at the crazed thought. Nakir is the lifeblood of Halos. If we don't save him, there won't be any more resistance groups. There won't be any more angels to fight Abaddon.

As we steer our horses down the bank, heading toward the Watchtower in the distance, I take out one of the two pieces that I made sure to bring along with me: Nakir's telescope. As I peer through it to get a better look at the tower, I fully understand why he wanted it.

Through it, I'm able to get a clear picture of the location of our final stand. Dark, obsidian walls at least a hundred feet high with fires sprouting all around it. I see how the earth around the Watchtower opens up into a pit of fiery innards, like I'm looking at the maw of a great fire beast.

The Watchtower, I realize, isn't just at the edge of the Door to Hell. It is smack dab at the gates, in a crater that is inaccessible to anyone without wings. Perfect for Demon Lords who still have their wings to fly to and from places, but not for three witches and a human that have no way of making that distance, especially with the proximity to the crater.

We'll have to cross that bridge when we get to it.

And hopefully there's a bridge.

Wordlessly, I put away the telescope into my near-empty saddlebags, and I snap the reins and dig my heels into Alion. He must get the seriousness of the situation, because he doesn't fight me. He just breaks out into a run and, bit by bit, increases his speed to a gallop.

I glare at the Watchtower, using it as my beacon as we head closer.

I'm coming for you, I promise Abaddon.

I'm going to kill you.

And I'm going to break the curse.

So what if we've been told this entire time that an angel has to kill the Demon Lord with an angel sword? We're at the end of our rope, and there's no other choice.

And I'm pretty damn sure that not even a Demon Lord can keep me from my goal.

"THERE'S NO WAY ACROSS," I mutter in frustration from our vantage point. "At least not that I can see."

We're really only about a mile away, just as the sun has

started peeking out over the horizon. Luck was on our side, as we hadn't encountered any more demonlings on our way to the Watchtower. Just us, our horses, and the hostile terrain. We alternated horses when we felt them get tired, and that seemed to do the trick.

All in about two hours of energy. Which means that we can get in there, get Nakir, and save the world.

Seems easy enough.

Except there's no way into the damn Watchtower.

"Let me see," Jennet asks desperately, taking the telescope from my hands. She sweeps it around to get a better look at the place, but I see from the pull of her mouth that she doesn't see anything different than I do.

A tall tower, a hundred feet high with windows that burn amber and red, like the core of it is made out of fire. The entire structure is flared at the bottom and rises to a point, like there's been a stake driven into the very earth by the heavens above.

The heat here is worse than anywhere else in the Door, from the fires that spew out of the crater before us, like lava. It's twice as wide as the tower is tall, effectively creating a moat out of the hot spots. The Watchtower sits in the middle of it, impossibly close to the heat, but that's what makes it such a great stronghold for a Demon Lord like Abaddon.

If this entire godforsaken desert is the Door to Hell, we just landed at its Door Step.

Jennet lowers the telescope and curses under her breath.

"Told you," I say blithely.

"That's impossible, though," Fatma says with a frown, speaking for the first time in a long while.

"What?" I ask.

She chews on her bottom lip, still appearing to be too frail to join us on this quest. "Abaddon must not be shielding the demonlings there," she says softly. "Because I can sense so many of them in there."

"Like, they're hiding out in there?"

She nods. "And demonlings don't have wings. I doubt Abaddon would fly all of them individually there."

She's making sense.

I look back at the Watchtower with renewed interest. There's another way, somewhere we aren't seeing. On the other side, perhaps, which would make sense, considering that humans would be coming from our side. With energy in short supply as it is, it's hard to justify checking all around the Watchtower.

But it's worth a shot.

I lead Alion around the lip of the crater. We try to stick to the shadows, but there's really not a whole lot we can do to hide. All we can do is move quickly.

Suddenly, I spot it.

"There!" I say, pointing as the other three follow my lead. "I see a bridge."

Bridge may be generous, considering that it consists of merely a narrow strip of land connecting us to an open door where I see a few demonlings guarding the entrance. There's barely enough room for one person to travel across it, and we certainly wouldn't be able to bring our horses on it.

Fatma gives a sad smile, looking physically ill. "Told you."

Maybe she's not completely lost.

"Okay," Jennet says. "Now what?"

"We tie up our horses," I say, dismounting and taking the reins to find a place to keep them while we go into the tower.

Unfortunately, this close to the Watchtower, there's really nothing here to tie them to. I pace around for a few moments, gritting my teeth.

I don't have the energy to look around too much. There

has to be something that works. I don't want to leave the horses loose, because they are our only way back to Derweze. But I can't spend all morning looking for a rock or something that can hold them.

"Fatma can stay here," Kerem offers, and the young witch whips her head his way. His gaze is soft as he looks at her. "Your gift allowed us to find this spot," he tells her gently. "And with so many demonlings there, you'll be more of a hindrance than anything."

Fatma's lips part, but I can tell that the fight left her before we went on this last leg. She doesn't want to contradict him. She doesn't want to say that she can do it, regardless. She knows she's at her very end.

"That's a good idea," Jennet agrees. She drops to the ground and hands Fatma the reins. "You'll do far better out here with the horses." She offers the younger woman a smile, giving her an encouraging pat. She presses a sword into Fatma's hand. "You'll be safer out here. Just keep an eye on everything to make sure that you aren't ambushed."

"Okay," Fatma replies, her voice tiny.

"Works for me." I sigh as I hand her my reins. I grab my yataghan and make sure that I have every available weapon that I can manage.

There's a lot, and I can't help but feel ridiculous as I signal to Kerem and Jennet to follow me as I run down the hill to the bridge. With every step, the heat from the crater gets more and more intense, and my body immediately becomes slick with sweat. The air itself becomes too hot and unbearable, and I wonder if we'll suffocate long before we make it.

A demonling roars, alerting its buddies that there are intruders on the bridge. Muscular, ugly creatures stream out of the building, running along the bridge to intercept us halfway.

The good news is, while they are counting on the bridge being a bottleneck for invaders, it's also one for them as well. Only one demonling can move forward at a time, and I use that to my advantage.

I hold my yataghan out, feeling its familiar weight, and I just start hacking, letting that now-familiar rage descend upon me. It's gotten me out of situations like this in the past—I need it more than ever now.

Blood flies, most of it not mine, and I find that the easiest way of getting them out of the way is to physically push them off the bridge and into the fires below. Charred demonlings smell like burned shit, and the scent makes my eyes water, which is a bigger deterrent than the fight on the bridge. My watery eyesight makes it hard for me to see them attack.

Jennet and Kerem are behind me, letting me do my work, knowing that if they try to help, they'll just get in the way and possibly hurt both of us.

Finally, after what seems like hours, but could only be minutes, we reach the end of the bridge. Here, the path widens, and we catch the demonlings on guard duty by surprise that we have made it across the bridge.

"Next time, make it wider, dumbasses," I growl to them as I slash through their bodies. The effect isn't as impressive as when Nakir used his angel sword, but there's something satisfying about them falling off into the crater below.

"Hurry!" I hiss, gesturing for Jennet and Kerem to come inside.

There are no more demonlings to greet us as we sneak in the front door, just an empty stretch of the Watchtower. The inside is hollow, with a ring around the perimeter the only walkway. A spiral staircase winds its way up to the roof. There are only two floors that I see: the floor we're on and the floor at the top.

The three of us cast a cursory glance around the place, poised and ready for the demonlings that Fatma said were in here.

None come to clash against us.

However, there is one thing that I do take note of.

Abaddon is horrible at decorating.

Maniacally, I laugh. The black walls are all bare. Then again, if he's afflicted by the same curse, he wouldn't be spending energy on something like that. It's the same reason I never repaired the recliners back at the Lodge or bothered to fix nonessential items around the property.

You simply don't have the energy, and there are far bigger fish to fry.

Seeing it in this grand scale, however, makes me realize just how big a problem it is for everyone involved.

"Do you think we need to go upstairs?" Jennet asks in a hushed whisper.

"Only one way to find out," I say honestly.

She flashes her eyes my way. "Yes, but what if it's a trap? We only have so much energy and…"

I nod, cutting her off. "We'll figure it out. For now, just trust that we're heading in the right direction."

It's the only reasoning I have. Kerem lets out an unimpressed sniff, but he doesn't have a better idea, so we head up.

We make our way up the spiraling stairs, our footsteps as soft as we can make them. No booby traps on the staircase. Good thing, too. I try to imagine myself slowing my breathing and heartbeat to make softer noises as we head up and up and up. We don't speak, only this panicked sensation of *must-keep-moving* driving us forward.

As we near the top, I wonder if we're going to be all right.

If there is enough energy in us to continue this fight if we're attacked.

Too late to worry about that now, I realize as we finally make it to the top floor. This is it. The end of the journey. If Abaddon isn't here, then we'll run out of energy before we can fight back.

If he is, then we have an entirely different set of problems on our hands.

Honestly, I'm not sure which one I'm hoping for.

But as I make my way to the landing, I see that demonlings are in something like bleachers, and as soon as they see my little group, they erupt into the raucous cheers. In the center of the large, circular room, I see Abaddon sitting in the center of the ring, expecting us. Like our surprise tactic didn't work out anyway. It's too soon after the demonling at the bridge gave the warning for him to have organized this.

He's planned this to showcase our demise to everyone.

Still, he does look impressed as we step out in front of everyone.

"Welcome to my home," he says grandly. "I must admit, you made it here quicker than I expected. I haven't even had a chance to follow through with the funeral."

Funeral?

Then my eyes fall on the still form behind him, lying on his back as if he might be sleeping. Candles with black flames are scattered throughout the room. It truly does look like we're at a funeral. The only thing that hints that something may be off is the giant sword still sticking out of the man's chest on the dais.

Nakir.

CHAPTER 28

"You haven't removed the sword?" I say dumbly. Of all the questions I could pose to the Demon Lord, I ask him this. But I can't tear my eyes away. It just seems… morbid. Grotesque. Like it's a trophy for him. "Why haven't you removed the sword?"

The angel's body lies on the ground, his eyes staring unseeing at the ceiling. He looks like he could almost be alive, laying there. I wish I were strong enough to remove the sword, give him a proper send off.

Abaddon looks at Nakir and shrugs in mock surprise, like he hadn't realized it was still stuck in there. "You caught us off guard."

I blink slowly, trying to process all of it. No, there has to be another reason. There has to be something else. It would have been hard for Abaddon to move Nakir with the sword like that. There is a purpose to it, because it seems so absurd.

Then it dawns on me like the hottest day here in the Door to Hell.

He's still alive.

It's hard to control my face at that realization. Nakir is still alive, and the only reason he's not moving is because his sword is keeping him from healing and getting up. Nakir told me that he's immortal.

And that hasn't changed despite the fact that there's a huge angel sword sticking out of his chest.

"I thought," I say, raising the level of my voice, "that you were as much a victim of the curse as we are. Why the big stage?" I gesture to the demonlings surrounding us. "Why put so much effort into something that won't matter?"

The Demon Lord's eyes narrow, but his smile doesn't falter. "Because I wanted to give my brother a proper sendoff. I'm as much a prisoner as you humans are. Sometimes you need to enjoy life as much as possible."

"Did you just call him 'brother?'" Kerem asks beside me, his voice quiet, contemplative. So subtle that I nearly miss it in my own thoughts.

I tear my eyes away from the angel's sword to give a hard look at Abaddon. I try to see the set of his jaw, the way he holds himself. Despite the obvious differences, from Abaddon having his leather set of wings to his red skin, their bone structure is similar. Their swagger is the same, that same kind of self-assured confidence that is not just because they're powerful beings.

Another thing that Nakir told me—Abaddon was like a brother to him when they both lived in heaven. Not that they *are* brothers, but it's technically still true, isn't it?

"Of course," Abaddon says slowly. "Isn't it obvious? Don't you see the resemblance?"

Shit, I really, really do now. How could I have missed it?

They're related. All this time, Nakir has been trying to kill his own brother. I hadn't realized it, hadn't thought on it. So many times I could have picked up on it, and…

I gulp back the lump in my throat, the feeling that we've stumbled onto something that makes all the difference. I can't believe it. Can't believe that he kept something critical like this from me and the Halos.

Can you blame him?

No. Does it really change things?

The answer to that is no as well.

I think back to the conversation I had with Nakir as we looked out at the Watchtower from so far away. Maybe he wanted to get a better feel for what Abaddon was doing out here. Maybe he wanted to feel closer to the brother he fell from heaven with. Nakir's love for a human changed him in certain ways and protected him from falling completely as a demon.

It's how Nakir knew that Abaddon is the source of the curse. He knew because he knew so much about his brother.

I look at the Demon Lord, trying to gauge how much energy he has left. Maybe he's been working just as hard as we have to get to this point.

I have maybe thirty minutes of energy left, which is the first time in a long time that I've nearly depleted it this early in the morning. I have to make it count, because we won't get another shot at breaking the curse.

But I have Jennet, in more ways than one.

I glance back at her and reach out my hand for her. "Lend me your strength," I whisper to her.

She wets her lips as her eyes widen, but she still takes my hand. I feel that now-familiar heat rise within me, of my energy coming back. I don't know how long she gives me, but I drop her hand suddenly, not wanting to take everything of hers. I know she'd give it to me.

Our gazes connect, and I wish I could give her one last kiss, tell her I love her one last time. But I'm out of time.

"Be ready," I whisper to both her and Kerem.

Jennet's eyes flash in worry, and I tear myself away before she can ruin the surprise.

I charge toward Abaddon with a yell, aiming my yataghan directly toward his heart. I feel a deep rumble reverberating throughout the entire room, and I realize that Abaddon is laughing at me, mocking me.

No, I have no chance against him with one-on-one combat. There's no way. But I'm not trying to kill him, not really. At the very last possible instant, I fake, twisting away from the Demon Lord, and run straight toward Nakir.

The last time I tried lifting Jan, my strength had given out and Abaddon had run me through. I have Jennet's strength whirling in my veins now. I make it to the sword and grasp at the hilt, trying with everything I have to get it to move.

Once again, it doesn't budge. My feeble humanity, the very reason Nakir likes hanging around earth, is going to kill all of us.

Fuck, fuck, fuck, fuck!

"What do you think you're doing?" Abaddon sneers before he rushes my way, raising his kilij in a downward strike. As I watch the blade fall, I see my own death, how there's no way I'll get out of this.

Maysa had been so sure it would end differently.

Well, in all those stories, you don't have a fuck-up for a hero. Which is exactly what I am. I failed everyone. I couldn't save the world.

After all, you're only human.

The clang of metal rings through my ears, and I blink in confusion to see Kerem blocking Abaddon's strike with his own sword. I'm still alive. Kerem stepped in to save me. The witch's muscles strain as he holds up the sword.

Abaddon snarls at us and raises his blade to strike again.

I have to try again. I grasp the blade and pull. *Pull, pullpullpull.*

It slides out. Barely, just barely, inch by inch, but as soon as it starts, it gets easier. I feel the cords in my neck strain against the sheer weight of the weapon, but I didn't take Jennet's power for no reason.

I try using everything I have to put it into this one last effort.

Please. For all that's good in this world, please.

I roar as the blade finally pulls free of Nakir's chest. It crashes to the floor beside me.

Now all he has to do is wake up. Wake up, dammit!

"*Kerem!*" Jennet screams, and I look up in time to see Abaddon slash him across his middle, disemboweling the male witch. The slick sound of blood and guts and everything else hits the dark floor, and I feel like my stomach drops there, too. Abaddon wastes no time and runs his blade through Kerem's chest, all the way to the hilt.

The witch stiffens around the sword, coughing up blood in the Demon Lord's face before he's kicked away. Kerem crumples in a heap.

Someone's screaming hoarsely, and I realize that it's Jennet. I grit my teeth, hating the hurt in her voice. Like Sena, she'll blame herself for Kerem's death.

It causes her pain.

And, Nakir's brother or not, I hate that Abaddon caused this for him.

"Jennet!" I yell. "Help Nakir!"

She whirls on me, her eyes streaming with tears as if she doesn't quite understand me. Her gaze falls on the now-freed Nakir. At the sword that lays behind him.

"No!" Abaddon roars. "Not you!"

The big demon tries to make it past me as she runs to the

fallen angel's side, but if there's anything I have left in me, I use it to meet the Demon Lord head-on. I actually catch Abaddon by surprise and land a blow on his cheek, a small cut that oozes thick black blood.

He turns murderous eyes on me. "You don't get it, do you, human?" he sneers at me.

Keep him talking. Keep him away from Nakir and Jennet.

"We're all prisoners here," Abaddon says to me, rounding on me like he's some sort of predator. "Nakir and I were cast down from heaven. And for what? Because he fell in love with a human woman? It nearly destroyed him. I was the only one who helped him. I was the only one who came to him. And how were we repaid?" He throws up his arms. "With a curse. And it's ruined everything!"

It takes everything I have not to glance behind me to see if Jennet made it to Nakir. To see if our last hope is awake.

Abaddon leans in closer to me, his breath hot and sticky, and I nearly gag. "Nakir lost everything. And God has the sense of humor to make *me* responsible for this curse. That my death would end it." His lip curls. "I refuse to be a pawn in this whole thing any longer."

He raises his sword, ready to hack off my head in one swipe—and I know he can do it, too, because he's that powerful. I wait for the inevitable end.

It doesn't come.

I open my eyes, which I hadn't realized I shut like a coward, and see Nakir standing between us, the sword of Jan in his hands as he parries, deflecting Abaddon's attack. There's still enough of a hole in his chest that I can see through to the other side. Somehow, Nakir is still standing. Somehow, he has the strength.

Somehow, he was healed.

Abaddon's eyes widen in disbelief. "Brother…"

Nakir smiles serenely. "Let's try this again."

And he meets Abaddon in the fight, more collected in his attacks, more assured of himself. I don't know if he knows he practically came back from the dead, but there's a calm over the fallen angel that hadn't been there the night before.

Now I chance a glance back to Jennet. And to my utter surprise, I see Kerem hoisting himself on the dais, his entrails dragging behind him on the floor. Jennet is with him, one hand on the witch and another where Nakir used to be.

It takes me a moment to piece together what happened. I think. Kerem must have healed Nakir, to do everything he could to make Nakir open his eyes and fight. Instead of healing himself, Kerem spent the last of himself bringing Nakir back to life.

And Jennet...Jennet used the last of her strength to give Kerem that energy.

"Fuck...you...de...mon..." Kerem mutters through a gurgle, spurting up blood, before the light leaves his eyes forever. He collapses forward, and his death rattle passes through his lips.

Jennet meets my eyes, but there's something off about her appearance, like she's become papery thin. She falls forward, and I drop everything I have to run to her side before she cracks her head on the hard ground.

She feels too limp in my arms as I hold her against me. I've held many people as the Hibernation overtook them, but this feels different. Like she went beyond her limits to grant Nakir this last boon.

"Jennet!" I shake her a little too roughly, but desperation makes me feel crazy things. "Jennet, wake up!"

I put my hands on her chest, her neck, her face, anywhere to see if I can find a pulse. Even if she's in Hibernation, I should be able to feel some sort of life within her. A heartbeat, the labored rise and fall of her chest.

There's nothing.

A low cry escapes my lips. "*No.*" Tears suddenly blur the entire world around me, my tears, but there will never be enough tears if Jennet died. She brought me back to life as a man. She brought out the good in me, reminded me why I joined the Halos in the first place so long ago. Reminded me why we keep fighting the good fight.

And now, she's gone. There's nothing in her to signify that she's alive. Just a limp broken husk of a body in my arms, too beautiful to go.

"Don't leave me like this. Jennet, don't leave me!"

Dimly, I hear Abaddon and Nakir fighting, but it doesn't matter anymore. Not with Jennet gone.

Did she know that she could give her life to someone along with her energy? It didn't matter to her, did it? She'd always been willing to sacrifice her life for others. In this last moment, she knew that she had to sacrifice everything for it.

My initial shock over, I rock her gently, smoothing down her hair and whispering to her to come back to me.

Even as I feel my own energy fading.

Time is up for me. Whatever bit I had taken from Jennet earlier—and I try to not dwell on the fact that if I hadn't taken it from her, she may still be alive—I'm about to fade, too.

Through my haze of grief and pain, I look up at the angel and the Demon Lord, still locked in a battle for supremacy. Suddenly, I feel too damn tired to care anymore. There's no point in this fight. Not with Jennet gone. I don't think I can live without her by my side.

She gave me purpose. And with that purpose gone...

The kilij goes flying, landing blade first into the ground

beside me. The steel twangs with the force of it. Abaddon has been disarmed by Nakir and holds up his hands placatingly, pleading with the angel.

"Nakir—" Abaddon starts, "you know why I did this. For you. Because you've been fucked by circumstance. Because someone has a bad joke that means you have to kill me for the sake of these humans. Don't you see? It was designed to turn us on each other."

Nakir looks at Abaddon for a long time before finally nodding. "The problem is, brother, you never realized why I was okay with it. I wanted to be here. And you let it twist you into this." He gestures helplessly. "I can't let you go on."

It's some part of a bigger conversation. I feel myself fall as Nakir swings the angel sword around—impossibly easy for him—and hacks it through Abaddon's neck, severing it in one go. The Demon Lord's head spins around once before sliding off its axis and falling to the floor.

Dead.

Dead.

Dead.

A whoosh of air escapes my lips, and I feel the sudden surge of energy pulse through my veins, enabling me to sit up again. I'm...awake... And I haven't fallen into the Hibernation.

I'm alive. Awake.

Nakir meets my eyes, and something like his own kind of grief passes beyond his eyes as he wipes the blade clean.

The rest of the room is silent as the fallen angel sweeps his eyes around the room. "The curse is lifted," he says simply. "Go live your lives."

I see the demonlings exchange uneasy glances with each other, as if doubting it to be true. After all, there could be no way, right?

After living my entire life with it, I don't even believe it myself.

But I could care less what an asshole gaggle of demonlings are doing. They should know better than to try anything right now.

After all, I'm barely hanging in there in a different way.

I look down at Jennet in my arms, and she still hasn't stirred. Like the curse being lifted hasn't changed her status.

"No," I say hoarsely. "No, the curse is gone, Jennet. You have to wake up! You have to——"

I feel the footsteps near me, and I look up as Nakir kneels next to me. "I tried a few times," he murmurs softly, "to break Abaddon's curse. My brother's curse. So much energy wasted. So much I could have done differently to tip the scales. She made all the difference, you know," he adds, gesturing with his chin to her still body. "It was arrogance that had prevented me from considering going to the witches before for help. To use their powers to help."

He looks at me, his expression grim. "A happy ending isn't just the work of one man," he says. A smirk plays across his lips. "It's the result of those who help you along the way. To remind you why you're fighting. And," he adds softly, coyly, as he takes Jennet's hand in his own, "every happy ending needs a kiss to wake up the princess from the spell. Or in our case, the curse."

For a crazed second, I think he means I need to kiss him. I lick my dry, chapped lips and look down at Jennet's form, still so beautiful and so still in my hands. I lean forward and kiss her, gently at first, but more insistent, more needy, as I beg her to come back to me, from wherever she is.

It starts as a flutter of movement in my arms, so faint that I don't even realize it's happening until I pull back to look at her. A muscle twitches in her cheek, and a shallow breath rocks through her lungs.

And she opens her eyes. I cry out her name, holding her to me. Unable to believe that a miracle as wonderful as this could have happened.

"Hey," she whispers. "Did we win?"

CHAPTER 29

The sun is high in the sky and the heat is as intense as ever as we emerge from the Watchtower. Tired, spent, and at our wits' end.

But alive and free of the curse.

I hadn't believed it could happen until now. That it was even possible. Because when the odds are stacked against you like they were against us, it seems like all hope fades.

Good thing you're too stubborn to give up.

"There you are," I mutter to myself. For a few blissful hours, I wondered if that voice had gone away with the curse. Turns out, it's still here. Like an old friend. Or like a permanent part of my conscience.

Jennet glances up at me, as I've spoken the words out loud, but doesn't say anything. A playful smile tugs at her lips, but she lets me deal with everything the way I need to.

I'll always be the broken man from three years ago, but bit by bit, I'm finding out that it's not the end of the world. I've faced that and lived to tell the tale. I look down at Jennet's hand in my own and give it a squeeze.

How wonderful and absolutely freeing it is to have her give me a squeeze back without calculating how much energy that will take.

Fatma is waiting for us with the horses, a look of utter disbelief on her features. She knows that she should be deep into Hibernation by now—after the hard ride we had this morning, we should all be at the mercy of the curse now.

"Did you…" she calls out to us, and she hesitates, like she can't find the right words to accurately convey the question. Like she can't believe what she's feeling herself.

Jennet nods, and a strangled cry escapes the younger witch's lips as she launches herself into the other woman's arms. Deep, wracking sobs shake Fatma's body as she buries her face into Jennet's shoulder, tired, worn-out sobs, and the two witches kneel to the ground, hugging each other as they cry.

A sense of guilt hits me then, for those we lost. Nury almost made it, could have had a happy ending with Fatma.

Not only him, but Kerem, who used his last moments to heal Nakir.

Rabia, who joined the Halos to fight for her dead family.

Murat, who had conceded that he lost in the game of love with Jennet.

Sena, who bravely walked through fire to protect us.

The first group of Halos and dreamers who had this crazy idea of taking on the Demon Lord themselves for the good of mankind.

I think of Emre, who, for his own reasons, decided to betray us. I'll never understand why, but I know what desperation looks like on a man. It's in the daily lists that are needed to make it through another day of life. It's in the fact that he's too tired and attached to cut down the tree that reminds him of his dead wife.

It's in his decision to join a suicide mission.

It's in the fact that I'm standing here now, after beating the odds, and wondering how I live a life without boundaries.

"I imagine the people of Derweze are probably still conserving their energy," Nakir says to me. I glance over at him. "They probably don't know what happened. They probably won't believe it for a long time from now."

"I still don't believe it," I murmur softly as I lock eyes with Jennet. She gives me a tired smile but turns away to take care of Fatma. I imagine Fatma will need a lot more help to get through these next few months, but it is possible to move on.

Now that we've done the impossible, I know that it can be done.

Nakir clasps my hand, a broad smile on his face. "Thank you," he says. "Thank you for not giving up on me."

"We had no choice," I say with a nonchalant shrug, although my heart swells with emotion. "It was either follow you here or die out in the Door." Neither decision was appealing.

"No." Nakir shakes his head. "Even beyond that. You joined Halos again after…after everything I put you through the first time."

I pause. Of course, I'm not going to tell him it's all right. So many hopes and dreams were shattered on that first trip. I nearly didn't make it out myself, but…

"I understand your reasons," I say simply. "I may not agree with them, but I understand."

A nod. "That's all I ask for."

Nakir takes the reins for his big bay Akhal-Teke and slings himself into the saddle.

I frown after him, my mind stuttering to a halt. "Wait… Where are you going?" When we had just accomplished everything we set out for?

The fallen angel grins down at us, his eyes sweeping from Fatma, to Jennet, finally to me. "You don't need an angel with you anymore," he says finally. "You don't need me around."

"But…" I fumble for words.

Nakir nods over toward Jennet and lowers his voice so he only speaks to me. "A long time ago, I fell from Heaven for the love of a woman. I was a broken man like you once, and now that I see you're able to put the pieces back together, then maybe…" His voice trails off as he looks at the two witches. "Then maybe there's something more for me after all this."

"So you're leaving?" My voice rises in anger, but the angel doesn't back down.

"What else are you going to do with an angel?" he asks amusedly. "You already have one there. *Two* by my estimates."

Jennet stills as she looks up at him, her jaw falling open. "What do you mean?" she asks.

But the fallen angel tilts his head toward us in good-bye, grinning like a madman. "I may be seeing you around," he says with a laugh. "Maybe."

He clacks the reins and gallops away. To where, I'm not sure.

But he has all the time and energy in the world to find out.

EPILOGUE

I t takes all too long to see the rays from the sunrise. I sit at the front of the Lodge, my back to the door, as I make sure that there's another sunrise on another day without the curse. The Devil's Teeth Mountains reach for the sky as it goes from midnight blue to a lighter blue streaked with yellow.

It's the signal of the start of a new day. I loose a breath and smile as I lean my head back, basking in the daybreak.

There's nothing more magical to me than living to see another day. Especially with the life I now have. The life I never thought I'd be able to live. Not after losing everything.

"Well, Maysa," I whisper. "I'm here another day. Without you. I wish you could have seen a world without the curse." I clench my fists and sigh. "Give Beste a kiss for me."

A low breeze whips around the desert, carrying with it a hint of fig in the air that tickles my nose. I close my eyes and inhale deeply, knowing that both Maysa and Beste are here with me. Welcoming another day. Telling me to keep living.

I'm glad you're doing all right.

"Hey," a voice murmurs behind me. I twist in my chair to look at my wife as she smiles at me from the front door. Jennet's hair is unbound as she looks down at me, her blue eyes soft. "Catching another sunrise?"

I nod to her. "Catching another day."

It's been eight months since Nakir killed Abaddon and the curse was lifted. Eight months since we traveled through Hell for a better future for everyone.

And so far, the future's been pretty damn good.

Barefoot, she pads over to me and wraps her arms around my neck. She presses her cheek up against mine and gives it a kiss. "They would have been proud of you."

"I know," I whisper. I put my left hand up and rub circles on her back with my thumb. I turn my head and catch her lips with mine. I feel her smile against me, and I wonder what I did to deserve an angel like her. Nakir may be a fallen angel, but Jennet is my own personal angel. She brought me back from the brink.

She's my whole world for the moment. And my world will be one person larger in about a month. Jennet and I—as responsible as we are—conceived out in the Door to Hell. A burst of life when it seemed like there was only desolation surrounding us.

Life has always had this funny sense of humor with me. But, hey, I'll take it.

"How's the baby?" I ask, putting a protective hand over her expansive stomach. "Still having trouble sleeping?"

"She's as feisty as her father, that's for sure," Jennet says with mock weariness.

I chuckle softly. "You're so sure it's a girl?"

She raises her eyebrow. "You dare doubt the wisdom of a witch?"

"*Former* witch," I correct her with a grin. That was one of the side effects we found out later of bringing her back. Jennet is no more a witch than I am. Her powers, which would be useless now, are nowhere to be found.

I asked her once if it bothered her. She told me she didn't mind. She may have defined herself as a witch in the past, but this is the start of a new era for her.

She makes a scoffing noise and playfully slaps my shoulder. "I still have the wisdom, even without my powers."

I pull her into my lap and wrap my arms around her burgeoning middle and put my head on her shoulder. She takes my hands and puts them directly on her stomach so that I can feel our daughter—because Jennet's *so sure* we're having a daughter—moving.

Ready to face the world.

I never would have believed I could feel this way almost four years ago. A dead man walking has been resurrected into something more.

A Lodge owner. A husband. A father. A man who is living day to day. And that sounds like everything I ever wanted in life.

"What's on today's to-do list?" Jennet asks, breaking into my thoughts. It's a game we play, where she tries to figure out if I have everything planned to the letter.

Funny thing is, when you don't have to worry about what you spend your energy doing, you're able to sit back and enjoy life as it's meant to be enjoyed. I haven't written a list in nearly seven months, and she knows this, too. It had been such a strange sensation to reach the end of the list and go, "Now what?"

So I stopped counting what I needed to do and just figured it out as I went. And the only times I pass out are when I've done too much living.

I'm sure that's what most of the people in my world are

experiencing these days. Bewilderment at days filled with anything you want, not with worry about where your energy will fail you.

I haven't told Jennet, but upstairs in our bedroom, deep within one of the drawers in our wardrobe, there's a notebook that has the last list I've ever written. I did it when I finally realized that I could break the habit.

1. *Love Jennet.*

That's it. That's all I need to be a happy man.

"Well, today," I say, giving her a slow smile, "I think I'm going to finish making up the nursery and help Yusup and the others prepare for today's check-ins."

That's right. After we made our way back to civilization, I rebuilt the Lodge on the same place where Maysa's father started the Lodge and where she and I spent so many happy days. I don't think of it as living in the shadow of the past. More like celebrating how life can go in so many surprising ways.

When I contacted my old staff to see if they wanted to join in, they couldn't say yes fast enough. And they have done everything they can to make the Lodge the best place possible. We don't get as many visitors now, because there's no need to split up the journey between Derweze and Merv anymore. But people will still stay a night. Say hi. Rest. Enjoy life.

Which is all we ask of them.

Fatma stops by on occasion to spend some time with Jennet, but I can tell that her heart isn't in living anymore. I hope she finds her way. That she doesn't have a second subconscious telling her things that make her doubt her actions. She's too young to have given up.

I hope she finds happiness.

"And you?" I ask, giving Jennet a smile. "What are your plans for today?"

"I think," Jennet says at length, "that I'll take it easy. Because we have a baby coming our way."

"Yes, we do," I say.

She only laughs.

"Hey, boss?"

We both turn to see Yusup standing in the doorway, looking ill at ease. He jabs a thumb back at the entrance of the Lodge. "Can you help me? We have a, uh, guest who won't move."

"What?" I ask as both Jennet and I get to our feet in shock. "Won't move?"

For a horrible second, I think the curse is back, that someone has fallen prey to Hibernation.

"Too much to drink last night," Yusup confirms, as if he caught our panic. "He probably needs a bath and some hair of the dog."

I blink before letting out a relieved chuckle. "I'll be right there," I say as I take Jennet's hand in mine. We leave the chair on the front porch of the Lodge, and we have the luxury of going out there every chance we get.

"I love you," I murmur to Jennet.

She beams at me. "I love you, too."

Life isn't meant to be experienced in short bursts. It's meant to be enjoyed all the time, because it's too precious not to.

Nakir gave me that chance. Maysa and Beste helped me reach that conclusion.

And I'm learning it as I go along with my family at my side.

ABOUT THE AUTHORS

Sci-fi junkie, video game nerd, and wannabe manga artist Erin Hayes writes a lot of things. Sometimes she writes books. She works as an advertising copywriter by day, and she's an award-winning New York Times Bestselling Author by night. She has lived in New Zealand, Hawaii, Texas, Alabama, and now San Francisco with her husband, cat, and a growing collection of geek paraphernalia. You can reach her at erin-hayesbooks@gmail.com and she'll be happy to chat. Especially if you want to debate Star Wars.

www.ErinHayesBooks.com

New York Times bestselling author Rebecca Hamilton writes urban fantasy and paranormal romance for Harlequin, Baste Lübbe, and Evershade. A book addict, registered bone marrow donor, and indian food enthusiast, she often takes to fictional worlds to see what perilous situations her characters will find themselves in next. Represented by Rossano Trentin of TZLA, Rebecca has been published internationally, in three languages.

www.rebeccahamilton.com

www.ingramcontent.com/pod-product-compliance
Lightning Source LLC
Chambersburg PA
CBHW031952240626
47153CB00003B/959